A LIFE OF
CONSEQUENCE

Published in paperback in 2015 by Sixth Element Publishing
on behalf of Beryl Robinson

Sixth Element Publishing
Arthur Robinson House
13-14 The Green
Billingham TS23 1EU
Tel: 01642 360253
www.6epublishing.net

© Beryl Robinson 2015

ISBN 978-1-908299-79-6

British Library Cataloguing in Publication Data. A catalogue record for this book
is available from the British Library.

Printed in Great Britain.

A LIFE OF
CONSEQUENCE

BERYL ROBINSON

To Caroline

Best Wishes

Beryl x

CHAPTER ONE
THE GUN

Washing the blood from her hands in the brackish water, she saw the red splatters on her dress. She rubbed at it manically. It would leave salt mark stains but that was better than his blood. Getting up from her knees, she saw him, laying on his front, head to one side, his arm outstretched as if trying to reach the hem of her dress. This side of his face looked as if he was asleep. Her first reaction was to move toward him, just to make sure he was dead, but she couldn't. She couldn't touch his grotesque flesh. He had never had any trouble touching her, violating her body over and over again. He was cruel, uncaring, ripping at her clothes as he demanded his rights. She shuddered as she imagined she could feel his coarse hands on her, hurting her. The thought made her retch.

A noise like the crack of the gun brought her to her senses. The horse and cart were still on the track, she would have to move them. She would have to get away, get inland before the tide turned. If she didn't, she too would be lost to the sea. Grabbing the skirt of her dress, she ran to where the horse had been waiting patiently.

"It's all right, Bobby," she said, patting the horse's neck gently. Her voice sounded normal but that was the last thing she felt. She had killed a man. Her husband, her cruel violent and drunken husband. She had killed him with her own gun. This time when her stomach rolled, she was sick. She would hang and the tiny baby she was trying to protect would die within her. She couldn't let that happen, she had already lost two babies before their time because of his brutality. This child growing in her belly must survive otherwise it would all be for nothing.

She struggled to climb onto the cart and took the reins in her shaking hands, encouraging the horse to walk on. She had to think. Where could she go? Where was she going? Returning to the house wasn't an option, someone would ask about him. His parents would make her life impossible nor could she return home to her parents, her father wouldn't allow that. More to the point, he would talk in the inn and she would be taken away. Forcing the horse into a trot, the only idea she could think of was to move the cart further along the marshes, far away from his body. She would leave the cart. Someone would find it and anyone searching would look for them in the wrong place. It would give her time, time to get away.

About a mile from the village of Thirlby was a turning onto the salt marshes.

"Come on, Bobby," she called as they moved toward it. In no time at all, she was there. Slowing down, she turned the horse, nodding, pulling. He didn't know this way and was getting anxious. They hadn't gone far before the path became boggy and she couldn't risk taking him any further. Getting down from the cart, her boots squelched in the black brownish bog. Turning the horse, talking quietly, she managed a quarter turn before the wheels became stuck. It would have been better if she could have backed the horse down the track but it was too late for that. She put the knitted blanket, bread, cheese and a small bag of oats into her basket. Her husband's rifle was attached to the back plate of the cart. She would have to leave it. Those who found the cart would have to believe they had both drowned. She fingered the small pistol in her pocket, her only comfort now that she was alone.

Bobby was getting more and more distressed as his feet continued to sink into the sucking mud. She untethered him from the cart and a few minutes later was walking him back toward the road, hoping that once they were on firmer ground she would be able to ride him without a saddle. He wasn't really a horse for riding but he had a gentle nature so she hoped he would let her sit on his back, otherwise she would have to rethink what to do.

It soon became clear that the idea of taking everything she had in the basket wouldn't work. She couldn't get on the horse whilst holding it, never mind hold onto the reins. She stuffed the items into her dress pockets and draped the blanket over Bobby's back. Throwing the basket toward the cart, she felt as though she was throwing away her old life.

She hitched up her dress, holding the reins in her left hand, and managed to somehow climb onto the horse's back. It wasn't ladylike, nor was it very comfortable without a saddle, but she hoped she could go some distance before nightfall. Urging Bobby on, she set off inland and as far away from the saltmarshes as she could get.

Bobby trotted quite happily as she used her knees to keep her balance. Her back was starting to ache already and a thought went through her head over and over again, 'I've killed a man,' like some kind of mantra. She didn't know where she was heading. She just let the horse have his head to go in any direction.

Coming back to the present as the horse slowed, she realised they had reached a fork in the road. The wooden signpost said Filby to the left and, to the right, Ormesby St Michael. She hadn't been to this part of the county before, she had never travelled very far in her life, but she did know that Ormesby St Michael had a church and a market. She didn't want to come into contact with anyone so she turned towards Filby as this seemed further inland and she hoped it was smaller.

Pushing Bobby onwards along the track, she hoped and prayed that they wouldn't meet anyone going in any direction. What would she say? It would seem odd, a strange woman riding alone and bareback on a horse. By taking a very narrow track, she hoped they would skirt the village. The path was not very wide so Bobby slowed considerably. In the distance, she saw a copse of trees so she pushed on toward them. Her throat was dry and she knew she desperately needed water.

After half an hour or so, they came to the edge of the trees. She

3

dismounted, continuing to skirt along the tree line. Stopping, she listened anxiously for any sounds but apart from birds going home to roost there was nothing. She cut across the undergrowth and found a path so narrow that she had to walk in front of the horse to stop them becoming entangled in brambles. Shuddering from the cooler air, she found a small stream and knelt to taste the water. It was fresh, not salty, so she allowed Bobby to drink. Cupping her hands, she could still smell the gunpowder mixed with the smell of the horse. She had thought she would hide in the woods for the night but it was too cold and damp. She took the reins in her hands and moved them on.

Just as she was beginning to despair at their predicament, she came to a gap in the trees. As it was almost dusk she thought this was as good a place as any to stop for the night. A large oak tree had fallen giving her somewhere to rest where she could see across the fields. The tree line would be on her left. Bobby could be tied to one of the branches out of sight of anyone on the horizon. She hoped that if anyone came behind her through the woods, she would hear their footsteps in the undergrowth.

Looking at her dirty chapped hands, her nails broken to the quick, her wedding ring caught her eye. She'd need to pawn it for money, she thought, to buy food and pay for somewhere to stay until she could find work. She lifted the hem of her petticoat and forced a couple of the small stitches apart, slipping the ring into the fold and moving it along the hem, so hopefully it would be safe there. At least she wouldn't be robbed for it, though that would be the least of her worries.

Taking out the small bag of oats, she put them on the ground for Bobby to eat and took the bread and cheese for herself. There wasn't anything to put any water in so she would have to do without. A small fire would have been nice to keep warm but she couldn't risk someone seeing the smoke. The setting sun made the temperature drop. Gazing at the sky, she thought it must now be around ten. Someone might be out looking for them by now. Maybe his body had already been found and perhaps they were looking for her. She was shaking as she wrapped the blanket around her head and body,

4

tucking her legs into her dress. She didn't know if the shaking was due to the cold or because of what she had done. She still couldn't believe that she'd done it. She had always thought she'd be relieved that he couldn't hurt her any more but now he was gone, she felt nothing but despair.

She didn't think she would be comfortable, let alone able to sleep but, strangely, she did.

CHAPTER TWO
THE TRAVELLING MAN

Waking just as it was getting light, Hannah stretched out her legs, body stiff, her bones aching with the damp air. Not only had she slept soundly but she had dreamed vividly, strange dreams of her childhood that left her feeling happy and sad at the same time. She had dreamed she was snuggling into her mother's back in a warm bed in the loft of their cottage. Her father would be asleep downstairs on a shaky down beside the fire. He always slept down there. She didn't know why, probably because he couldn't climb the ladder to the bedroom when he was in drink. The cottage was little more than a hut really. It had one up, one down and had belonged to her mother's family. They grew their own vegetables and had chickens for the eggs. Her father worked with horses on Holdham Hall estate. He would often be away for weeks if the master was around. His wages were paid quarterly when her mother would walk her to the gates of the hall for his money, otherwise it would be spent in the Black Bull which would leave them without any for food.

She didn't know how her parents had met, nor why they married. They never seemed happy. Bits of the dream lingered. She had dreamed she was hiding upstairs, listening as her mother and father screamed at each other. It had always been that or an icy silence. Whatever it was, she had to keep out of her father's way. He would often strike her if she got too close so she huddled upstairs waiting for him to be gone. She would hear a door slam and the house would be quiet. She remembered creeping down the stairs in the dream and then it was just her and her mother again in a lovely warm house. Her mother cuddled her, brushing her hair before the fire. That was the part of the dream she wanted to hold on to.

Oh, how she loved her mother. She wished she could reach out and touch her. Her mother understood what Hannah's marriage would be like. That's why she had given her the small pistol, hoping she would never have to use it. The bluish grey of the barrel was in sharp contrast to the mother of pearl handle. It was a ladies' gun which could be hidden in a purse but where her mother had got it, Hannah didn't know. There hadn't been time to ask.

Patting Bobby on his rump before moving toward the bushes, a smell of smoke reached her nostrils. She listened for any sound as her fingers wrapped around the handle of the gun for protection.

Picking up the folds of her dress in both hands, she pulled the material taut, in the hope that she could move toward the smoke without disturbing the undergrowth. She stopped about ten yards away and put her hand out to steady herself. The scene intrigued her. It could have been a painting, just like the ones she had seen once before in the big house. With his back to her was a man with the blackest hair she had ever seen, tied at the nape of his neck in a ponytail. His shoulders were broad. He seemed to be quite tall though this was difficult for her to determine while he was sitting on a stone tending to whatever he was cooking. Two dogs were sitting close to him, ears pricked alert to his every move. One was a large grey wolfhound. The other a small white and brown terrier. Both were mesmerised by their master who was talking to them but she was too far away to hear what he was saying. Further away eating grass was a piebald pony. His markings made him a pretty horse. His face and rump were black with white legs and a large white spot over his neck and shoulder. There was also a lacy effect on the back leg nearest to her. What surprised her was how well kept all the animals seemed; they were certainly well fed. The cart was a house on wheels. It looked like a wooden shed with a door in the middle and two steps in front of the opening. It was smaller than the shepherds' huts she had seen at lambing time.

Leaning forward to get a better look, a twig snapped under her foot. Hannah held her breath.

"Care to join me for breakfast?" he asked without turning.

Both dogs ran toward her. Reluctant and scared but too hungry and thirsty to resist, she moved to meet the dogs and their master.

"Grab a pew," he said, pointing to a log opposite him at the other side of the fire. "Wondered how long it would take for you to find me."

"You knew I was here! How?" she asked in amazement.

"Saw you sleeping, dead to the world you were, girl. Lucky for you it was me who came across you or you could have been murdered in your sleep," he said.

Tears pricked her eyes as he spoke, staying on her long lashes like morning dew on a blade of grass. She managed to compose herself before they escaped down her cheeks. He passed her a mug of sweet, strong tea and she wrapped her hands around it gratefully.

"Eggs, mushrooms and bread," he said, putting each item onto a tin plate.

She nodded gratefully. Neither spoke as they ate and drank, and even the dogs lost interest, resting by their master.

Eventually he broke the silence, saying, "Well, what's a pretty young thing like you doing out in the woods on your own? Where are you heading?"

"I'm not on my own," she responded. "I've got Bobby with me."

"That'll be the same horse that accepted the carrot from me last night without even a murmur, is it?" He smiled, his dark brown eyes lighting up. "I'll ask you again, where you heading."

"North." It was the first thing that came to her mind.

"Must be your lucky day. I'm going to Kingsmead if that's anywhere near where you are heading, if you care to join me," he replied. "More tea?"

She made to stand up. "I must see to Bobby."

"Sit down. I'll bring him here then you can give me an answer." He moved off before she could reply.

What should she do? She was frightened, on her own, and apart from the gun had no means to protect herself, no food. He could be a murderer. Well, so was she. Hadn't she killed her husband yesterday? He must have been found by now. They'd be looking for her, surely. They'd be looking for a woman alone with a horse. If she joined this man, it would give her time to hide and think. She didn't know if she could trust him but she made up her mind. She had no choice.

By the time he returned with Bobby, she had washed all the utensils and stacked them on the first step. She left the used water to put out the fire.

The man held up her blanket. "Is this all you have with you? In a rush, were you? The name's Daniel. Yours, partner?" he said smiling.

"Hannah, partner," she replied, returning his smile.

In no time at all, he packed up all his belongings, his horse was between the shafts and Bobby fastened behind the cart.

"Up, Laddie, Spot," he called as the dogs jumped into the cart before curling up on the clippie mat on the floor.

Off they went at little more than a walking pace. Hannah had to curb the urge to try to hurry him. Every step was taking her further away from her husband, her dead husband. Neither of them spoke for hours and hoping he had forgotten she was there, she didn't move. Her legs were starting to cramp up. He whistled occasionally but didn't look at her. Finally she had to shift her position, stretch her legs.

"How far are we expecting to go today, Daniel?" she asked, looking straight at him.

"We'll be doing about fifty miles till we get to Bogs End Farm. Spend a couple of days there helping out. The lady stocks me up with supplies and it gives Pinto here a couple of days rest." He nodded in the direction of his horse. "I do some work for her. She might be able to find you something to do to pay for your board and lodge. Alright with you, Hannah?"

She nodded.

They slipped back into a comfortable silence. She didn't feel the need to break it but she looked around at the ever-changing landscape. The further away they travelled, the more relaxed she became. Her shoulders became less tense. Her hands sat comfortably on her lap. Until she stopped, she hadn't realised that she had been picking at her dress with her fingers.

They stopped briefly to give the horses water, but she only managed a short walk to stretch her legs before they were on their way again. By mid-afternoon they were on a well used track. Pinto snorted and picked up his pace. He seemed to know where he was going.

CHAPTER THREE
BOGS END FARM

Hannah spotted what appeared to be two men in a field before the entrance to the farm. Both of them looked up and waved.

Daniel shouted, "Your ma in the house?" Not waiting for a response, he turned toward a cutting which took them into a yard. The dogs jumped down before the cart had even stopped, running back toward the field.

"Let's get these horses stabled then we can go and I'll introduce you to the lady of the house," Daniel said, moving to unfasten the harness on his horse.

Hannah untied Bobby, patting his neck and speaking quietly to him. "We'll be okay, lad, and you'll be nice and warm in here."

Daniel threw her blanket to her saying, "Here, put this over him. We can come back later to feed and water them."

The lady of the house was a small wiry woman with white grey hair in a single plait which reached to the small of her back. Her skin was tanned and smooth, which made it difficult to ascertain her age.

The lady hugged Daniel like a prodigal son before turning to Hannah. "Found yourself a wife, you scoundrel?"

"No, no, don't go making assumptions. This is Hannah. We are both travelling to Kingsmead so thought we would travel together."

Daniel's tone prevented the lady asking any more questions. Instead she held out her hands toward Hannah and said smiling,

"I'm Mrs Whisker and you are very welcome in my home. Any friend of Daniel's is a friend of mine."

Hannah couldn't help but smile. There was a warmth to the lady and a bright sparkle in her eyes. It was comforting to feel so welcome.

Mrs Whisker turned back to Daniel. "Did you see the girls in the field?"

'Girls?' Hannah thought.

"Aye I did that. What are you feeding them? They get bigger every time I see them." Daniel laughed.

"You're not wrong there, Daniel. Hope and Grace, what possessed me to call them that, there is no hope nor grace in either of them." Mrs Whisker joined in the laughter. "Eeh, lass, where are my manners? Come and sit yourself down."

"Could I freshen up first, Mrs Whisker? I feel quite dirty after the journey," Hannah asked quietly.

"Of course," the lady said. "Come with me, I'll show you where."

Mrs Whisker took her to a small lean-to and left her to it. Looking around, Hannah saw a cold water tap, a bucket, a piece of carbolic soap and a square of rough sack hanging from a nail. Rubbing the soap between her hands to try and get a lather, she found it difficult as the water was so cold. Instead she swilled her face, drying it on the hessian sacking. Her hands moved to the gun in her pocket. It was the first time today she had even thought about it. She drew her thoughts away from the violence of that moment when she had pulled the trigger and murdered him, thinking instead back to her mother and the warmth and protection that gave her.

Returning to the kitchen, Daniel and Mrs Whisker were talking animatedly. Both glanced toward her as though they had forgotten she was there. The table was now laden with plates full of bread, cheese, scones, butter and jam. A large brown teapot sat next to a jug of creamy milk.

"Come on, lass, help yourself. The evening meal won't be for a few hours yet," Mrs Whisker said, pouring out a mug of strong black tea.

Draining his cup before getting to his feet, Daniel winked at Hannah. "I'll go and sort the horses out while you ladies have a chat about me."

She had the urge to grab him, beg him not to leave her with this small wiry woman. She was frightened any kindly words would cause her to cry or speak about what she couldn't get out of her mind.

He no sooner went out of the door than she spoke. "Can I do anything, Mrs Whisker? Prepare vegetables? Clear the table?" She knew she was rambling but she didn't want a barrage of questions she wouldn't be able to answer.

"Aye lass, take the cups and plates to the sink. Can you set the table for six? We can have a little chat and a rest before the girls get home."

Thankfully, Mrs Whisker didn't ask any questions but sang quietly as she busied herself.

The light was fading when Daniel returned with the two girls. She stared at them, closing her mouth when she realised it was open. The two girls were in fact the figures she had thought were men in the fields earlier in the day, pitchforking hay. They were both tall, towering over their mother. Her own mother would have called them big boned. Their backsides were almost as big as they were tall but their bosoms had somehow been replaced by muscle. Their arms were used to physical work but what struck her most was that they looked identical with the same hair, cut short which she had never seen on a woman before. Their facial expressions and mannerisms were exactly the same. She was fascinated.

"These are my girls, Grace and Hope, though even I can't tell them apart," Mrs Whisker said, nodding toward them.

The girls' round faces wobbled as they nodded in unison. They both wore men's trousers tied at the waist with string and dark coloured long sleeved shirts tucked into the trousers. Their sleeves were rolled up above the elbow. They had obviously washed, though their short broken nails were ingrained with dirt.

Realising everyone was looking at her, Hannah smiled at the two of them. "Nice to meet you, I saw you working hard in the field earlier," she said.

The ice broken, the girls pushed each other, saying together, "Must have been me you saw, she's the lazy one," as they pointed at each other.

Hannah sat next to Mrs Whisker at the table, the girls opposite, with Daniel sitting at the head at one end. The other end was empty even though she had laid a place. She assumed that must be Mr Whisker's seat. Daniel seemed comfortable in this family's company, the conversation easy. They talked about the price of animal feed and the small weekly market where they sold food. Daniel asked which animals were for slaughter the following day. The two girls cried at the thought of their two beloved pigs being no more. They sobbed even louder when Mrs Whisker called them no good farmhands.

The meat and vegetables had been cooked to perfection in the bottom of the oven. On top was something Mrs Whisker called a dumpling which Hannah had never tasted. It was delicious. An apple pie followed with cream from the milk.

"Mrs Whisker, I have never tasted anything so nice in my life," she said. She didn't think she had ever felt so full either.

"Flattery won't get you out of the washing up." Daniel laughed and the girls joined in.

Once the table had been set for the following day, they all sat on the two settles which had been moved from the fireside and placed either side of the still warm cooker. Mrs Whisker picked up her embroidery while the girls took up a pack of cards. "Do you want to play? Daniel? Hannah?" they both said.

Shaking his head, Daniel said, "No chance. You two cheat. I'll just have a smoke of my pipe and a think."

Hannah shook her head. "I don't know how to play but I'll have a go if you show me."

The girls were at pains to show Hannah the game, both talking at once but there was joy in their faces as they tried to explain. It was only after a few hours had passed that Hannah realised she hadn't thought of her troubles for most of the evening.

It soon began to get dark so Mrs Whisker lit a couple of lamps, giving one to the girls as they headed off to bed.

"Old as they are, the daft pair still share a room," Mrs Whisker remarked. "I've put you in the small room, Hannah. Daniel, you know you are welcome to put a shaky down on the floor in here. It's warm but I know you like to be near the animals."

"Aye," was all he said, putting on his boots.

"I don't want to be any trouble, Mrs Whisker," Hannah said. "I can sleep in the spare stable."

"Will you offend us by refusing the hospitality after stuffing yourself with me food?" Mrs Whisker asked sternly.

Both Mrs Whisker and Daniel looked at her before laughing. "Come on lass, I'll show you the way. Night, Daniel," Mrs Whisker said, picking up the small lamp.

"Goodnight, Daniel," Hannah said quietly.

"Goodnight, partner," he replied, still laughing.

Hannah followed Mrs Whisker up the stairs to a small room. After lighting the candle which was on a small side table beside the bed, Mrs Whisker turned to Hannah and gave her a hug before leaving.

Once the door closed, the tears fell in tracks down her face. She really didn't know why she was crying. Not for her dead husband, she was sure of that. These people she had just met had shown her more kindness in one evening than anyone other than her mother. They seemed happy, and had somehow managed to make her laugh when she never thought she would laugh again. She didn't think she had been shown so much care, even as a child. Her in-laws had shown her nothing but disdain, treating her like a slave from early morning until last thing at night. She could have coped, would have coped, if a bigger nightmare hadn't started when she retired to bed. They never acknowledged the black eyes, split lips, bruised face, nor the nightly screaming. His mother never gave her a kindly word, they were both petrified of their son. Their son, and her now dead husband.

She was a widow expecting a child. How she was going to survive, she didn't know. She had to otherwise it would have all been in vain. Holding back the sobs which threatened to wrack her body, she looked around the room. On the bed lay a clean but old and frayed nightshirt which must have belonged to Mrs Whisker as it wasn't wide enough for the girls. On the highly polished dressing table was a ewer of warm water, a matching bowl and a small tablet of lavender soap. She would have loved to wash her hair with the soap but it was too late, it would never dry and she was tired.

Feeling really daring, she stripped naked, washing every part of her body in the warm water before drying it on the fresh towel. Looking at the small curve of her stomach, she prayed this child would survive. She would love it and that was all that mattered. Then she pulled the nightshirt over her head before opening the curtains. She climbed into bed and snuggled in, looking out at the night sky where the stars were twinkling. The cotton sheets were cool on her legs, her head comfortable on a soft pillow. She felt calm for the first time in days and she fell into a deep sleep.

Hannah opened her eyes slowly. The sun was shining in through the small window. A rainbow was dancing on the wooden floor. Closing her eyes again, she could still smell the hint of lavender soap on her skin.

Too soon though, a tapping on the door brought her to her senses.

"Yes," she called, "I'm awake."

Mrs Whisker pushed open the door, a mug of tea in her hand. "There you are, lass, it's going to be a lovely day. When you are ready, I've left some clothes for you and I've warmed some water so you can give your hair a good wash," and with that she turned and walked out of the room, closing the door quietly behind her.

Picking up the lavender soap and towel, Hannah looked around for her clothes, the ones she had discarded on the floor last night. She had left them in an untidy pile on the floor like rags. They weren't there. Panicking, she couldn't think where they could have gone, but neatly folded on the back of the chair was a green pinafore, a lighter green blouse, white petticoat, bloomers and stockings. Sipping the tea, she tried to think what to do. She would have to get away from the farm before anyone found the gun in the pocket of her dress, wherever it was.

Downstairs, she filled the bucket with warm water before going into the yard to wash her hair by the standpipe. She felt vulnerable, expecting someone to shout at her, call her a murderer. Kneeling on the floor, she tipped her hair forward into the bucket, lathering the soap as she massaged her head. It hurt where she had been yanked off the cart by her husband, just a few days ago.

Rinsing her hair in cold water, a shiver ran down her spine. Her head felt as though it would crack with the shock of the cold on her skin. Wrapping it tightly in the towel, she emptied the water from the bucket, turned and saw her clothes blowing innocently on the line. Oh God, she felt sick. This was worse than when she had shot him.

"Oh God help me!" she whimpered. She couldn't run, she didn't know where she was. Where could she go?

The kitchen door opened. Mrs Whisker called to her. Neither spoke as she headed in to go upstairs, her heart pounding in fear.

Back in the small bedroom, the clothes were a little short, her ankle was showing but no matter she would have to make do. Brushing her hair with the silver brush from the set on the dressing table, her hand was shaking violently. She felt clean, her body was clean but her mind was in turmoil. She would have to leave. This family, this loving and caring family, could not be accountable for harbouring a murderer.

As she walked slowly down the stairs, she could hear the voices of Mrs Whisker and Daniel. Pausing, she tried to listen to what they were saying. "She is with child, Daniel. Is that child yours?" she heard Mrs Whisker ask.

"What? No. What child? No, I didn't know," Daniel replied. "Are you sure about that? I told you I found her sleeping in the woods."

"There's summat not right. What is that black bruise she has on the back of her neck? You'll have to talk to her, Daniel. I don't like it, I don't like it one bit." Mrs Whisker looked round angrily as Hannah entered the kitchen.

"I owe you both an explanation," Hannah said, looking down in horror at the gun and the wedding ring laid out side by side on the table in front of them. "Please can I sit down?" she asked, gripping a chair. "I think you will both need to sit also."

And then she told them her story about her parents, her father selling her into marriage at sixteen. She had miscarried before, a couple of times but, yes, she was now pregnant. She explained how her mother had given her the gun, about the beatings and the rape at the hands of her husband. The tears flowed. Mrs Whisker joined in as she told them she had murdered her husband because she couldn't take anymore. She told them about how she had left his body on the marshes hoping he would be washed out to sea and how finally she had come upon Daniel the following day.

When she had finished, her head was in her hands. No one spoke. The silence seemed to last for hours and she thought they had walked away, leaving her alone. When she looked up, they were both still sitting there looking directly at her. It was difficult to ascertain what they were thinking. There was a mixture of anger and sympathy in their eyes. Mrs Whisker had tears in hers.

"I'm sorry, Daniel, Mrs Whisker, I'll leave immediately if you just point me in the direction of the nearest town." Her voice was shaking at the thought of being thrown out and alone.

"Let me think, let me think, girl." Mrs Whisker was almost shouting. "It happens in marriage. Didn't your mother tell you? No reason to kill a man, there are other ways. Listen to me, I don't want my girls knowing about this. The less people know, the better. Do you agree, Daniel?"

"Aye right, look where my kindness has got me. Knew something wasn't right. A young girl out on her own with nothing with her," he replied.

"Hannah, go and bring your clothes in then take these things up to your room. Go on, quick, before the girls come in for their lunch." Mrs Whisker almost spat the words in her fear and anger.

By the time Hannah returned to the kitchen, Daniel had gone. Her mind was again in a state. In some ways she wished Mrs

Whisker would ask her something, get her to explain. Shout even, but apart from giving her an apron, a pan and vegetables to chop, she didn't utter a word nor did she sing.

At four o'clock, his work finished, Daniel went back into the kitchen where Hannah was sitting with Mrs Whisker, tea with bread and cheese set out before them on the table.

Hannah looked up. "You won't report me, please?" she said. "I never meant to do it, never meant to run away. I just panicked. I couldn't take any more beatings."

Daniel stared at her. Her hair shone. It was a colour he'd never seen before, not brown nor auburn, but the colour of autumn leaves with a rich red running through it. It enhanced the sparkle in her large brown eyes that were still wet with tears. Her face was almost childlike, her voice pitiful and pleading. She was still a child despite being married. Had never had a chance. No one should have to live like that, he thought. He couldn't judge her. After all, he wasn't innocent either.

"What do you intend to do when you get to Kingsmead?" he asked. "Have you anyone there?"

"No, no one. I thought I might be able to sell Bobby or my wedding ring to pay for lodgings until I found work," she replied.

"What happens when the baby comes?" Mrs Whisker said. "How will you manage then? Jumped out of the frying pan into the fire, lass."

"I don't know. I never thought that far ahead," said Hannah. "I just couldn't take any more. He would have killed me eventually and what would have happened to my baby then?" Wringing her hands, she continued. "You will still take me, won't you, Daniel? Please. I'm begging you."

"You don't know what you're asking," he replied. "I'm not responsible for you but I do feel you need help. Life won't be a bed of roses trying to manage on your own with a bairn."

"Well, she can't stay here," Mrs Whisker interrupted. "Someone will find out. Lord knows we don't get many visitors but gossip spreads in small villages. You need to get further away. Daniel, you've got to take her with you. She can't stay here."

He nodded and that was the end of the conversation.

The evening passed the same way as the night before. The girls came in and they all ate a hearty meal before they retired.

There was a tap on her door just as Hannah was about to blow out the candle. It was Mrs Whisker, carrying a sheet, a couple of pillowcases and a large towel which looked new as well as a woollen blanket.

"Are you any good at sewing, lass?" she spoke quietly. "Maybe you can use these to make things for the baby and a change of underclothes for yourself."

"My stitching is quite neat though I'm not sure I could make something. It's very kind of you," she replied.

"Well anyway, take them, Hannah." She stroked Hannah's hair as she spoke. "Eeh lass," she said and with that she left the room.

Leaving the curtains open again, Hannah fell into a fitful sleep. She could see him standing in the field holding a pitchfork in his large fat hands.

He staggered closer to the house until she could see his face. One eye was missing, his cheek red, his mouth open at a strange angle. He looked straight at her through the window. She could feel his hands grabbing at her body. The blood curdling scream rose louder as she tried to fight him. Hannah screamed louder and louder as the door burst open.

"In the name of God, girl, what's going on?" Mrs Whisker stood there in her nightdress, her grey hair plaited to one side.

Hannah sat bolt upright. It was just a dream.

Mrs Whisker sat beside her and put her skinny arms around her shoulders, rocking her back and forth until she could feel herself calming and the crying stopped.

Leaving the lamp burning low on the dressing table, Mrs Whisker closed the curtains. Kissing Hannah's forehead, she said, "Get some sleep, he can't hurt you now."

Laying still in the soft light of the lamp, Hannah tried to calm herself, breathing deeply as her sobbing eventually subsided. It was a nightmare, nothing more.

He's gone, he's gone.

Eventually her eyes closed and she slept soundly.

CHAPTER FOUR
MOONDANCE

The following morning Hannah was woken before it was light. Daniel had already packed up the cart. The horses were ready to go. Mrs Whisker pushed some bread and bacon wrapped in paper into her hands, along with a tin of tea.

"Eeh lass, take care of yourself," she said and hugged Hannah so tightly she could barely breathe.

"Bye, Hannah," the girls said together.

She watched as Daniel put his arms around the girls as far as he could and said, "Bye, you big soft lumps. Don't be taking no lip from your ma." He let go of the girls and smiled at Hannah before moving toward the door.

"Don't forget to thank your sister for those waistcoats she sent us for Christmas," Mrs Whisker called after him.

He raised his hand as he waited to help Hannah up the step onto the cart. Waving until her arm ached, there was a tension in her shoulders, as though bracing herself for what would happen next. How she would have loved to have stayed at Bogs End Farm, cocooned in their happiness and contentment. She wouldn't have cared about the outside world even if she never saw anyone else. Her child would have been brought up in a happy home. Peaceful... that was the word. The farm was peaceful.

As the cart trundled along, there was an atmosphere between her and Daniel. She could almost touch it. He was angry with her, she knew that. Eventually she could stand the silence no more. "I didn't know you had a sister, partner," she said, trying to lighten the mood.

"There's a lot you don't know about me, Hannah, and it's probably for the best." He didn't turn to her as he spoke.

They didn't speak again and the silence was strained, even when they stopped to water the horses. They ate their bread and bacon without speaking. He didn't speak when he handed her a mug of lukewarm tea. It was the same all afternoon.

As the light was just beginning to fade, Daniel pulled off the track into a gap in the trees which was wide enough to turn the cart. He tended to both horses as the dogs jumped down from the cart, sniffing around the undergrowth.

Needing to be useful, Hannah walked around the clearing collecting wood and kindling to make a fire. Daniel had already unpacked the pots and pans when she returned.

Picking up two buckets, one for the horses and one for herself and Daniel, she set off toward the sound of water. It was a brook filling a pool. She would have loved to have taken off her shoes and stockings to feel the cool water rush between her toes but thinking better of it, she bent to fill up the buckets. They were both heavy and, even though Daniel turned as she stepped into the clearing, he didn't help her.

Soon the water was boiling and two heaped spoonfuls of tea went into the metal pot. Putting it to one side to brew, Daniel placed two pork chops into the frying pan allowing them to brown before turning. Once they were cooked, he put them onto a plate and broke two eggs into the pork fat. It was delicious. She ate hungrily, mopping up the pork fat on her plate with a piece of bread.

Once they had finished eating, Daniel lit his pipe with a twig from the fire before heading toward the back of the cart. Feeling dismissed, Hannah gathered up the pots and pans, taking them to the stream to wash.

This time she did take her shoes and stockings off. Sitting on the bank, she shivered as her feet slowly entered the cool water. She sat with her dress up above her knees to keep it dry, and head back, eyes closed, she savoured the feeling of numbness in her feet.

Daniel walked further down the track with both dogs running on ahead. He stopped as he saw her sitting on the grass by the pond. Light was filtering through the trees, dappling the water. It sparkled like fairy wings darting among the late dragonflies. The light was doing a moondance around her head, giving her a halo. The picture seemed frozen in time, of innocence, purity and light. She looked so childlike. Daniel could imagine her squealing in delight as the cold water touched her feet, splashing, trying not to wet the hem of her dress. The reality wasn't like that, Daniel thought. She wasn't a child; she was a married woman, a widow and murderer. She was also pregnant and not for the first time.

He turned, leaving her with her thoughts, whistling for the dogs before returning to the fire. He would have to get rid of her, he must distance himself or they could both be in danger. The parcel he had picked up on his walk was now hidden in the bottom of the cart before she returned.

Daniel had given her his narrow bed so he settled himself with the dogs close to the fire where they fought to get closest to the heat. He loved being in the open air with a night clear enough to see the stars.

Hannah had been asleep but she heard a tap, tap, tapping. It sounded like a loud clock ticking, the one in the hallway of her husband's house. She was back in that place again, her husband climbing the stairs, the sound of the metal latch opening the bedroom door. The shadows in the room changed as the door widened. The scream stuck in her throat, she was gasping for air.

"Nooo, noooo." Her garbled groan was getting louder.

His face was on top of hers, she could smell his foul breath. She thought she was going to die. He was here. He had found her.

"It's pouring down out there," she heard someone say. Daniel. It was Daniel. "We'll have to bed down on the floor," he was saying.

"Hey, what's the matter, Hannah? Hannah?" he continued as she sobbed, trying to catch her breath.

"I thought it was him. I thought he had come to get me," she cried.

Daniel put his hand toward her but pulled back as she cowered, shrinking back. She grabbed the blanket to her breast.

"No one is going to hurt you while I'm here. Now try and get some sleep if you can. Though the smell of wet dog won't help," he said, pushing the dogs out of the way to make some space for himself.

The rain continued throughout the night and into the next day. Hannah ran to the stream to fill up the can with fresh water and splashed her face, drying it on her dress before running back to the cart. Her boots and the hem of her dress were wet and muddy but there was nothing she could do. Laddie and Spot were already sitting in the cart. Daniel indicated she should do the same. He was wearing a moleskin cape and hat, the rain trickling down his neck.

They set off along the muddy track. They didn't stop to eat, there wasn't any point as they wouldn't be able to light a fire, she thought.

The silence between them continued. The noise of the rain helped as they wouldn't be able to hear if they did talk. The rain and movement seemed to lull her, her mind blank. The tension of the previous night seemed to ebb away with the passing miles. Wrapping her shawl tightly around her shoulders, she watched the steam rising from the horse. Poor Bobby trotting behind the cart.

She thought it strange that they had never met anyone on their travels but no matter, it was probably for the best. Stopping to rest the horses, she looked around for something to eat. Her belly was rumbling so she involuntarily rubbed it. Picking up the last of the now dry bread, she sliced it thinly. It would take some chewing but at least it would last longer. Taking the pork dripping which had been drained from the frying pan last night, she spread it on the slices. The fat was white against the grey of the bread, the brown jelly with small pieces of pig's blood in it.

Daniel sat on the pallet while she carefully poured water into two mugs. Sitting side by side, almost touching, chewing, the pork fat helped them to swallow the bread. The cold water coated the back of her throat with grease. "Delicious," she said.

"Listen, there is a change of plan," he said quickly.

"Change of plan? What do you mean?" she asked. "I didn't know we had a plan."

"Don't ask any questions, just listen. The less you know the better," he continued. "We'll get to Dealham in a couple of hours. I'll have to drop you on the outskirts. We don't need to be seen together. It will be safer for you." Reaching around his neck, he took off a plaited cord, and handed it to her.

"Go to the Green Man and ask for the owner. If he is there, show him it. Will you do that, Hannah? Tell him you will work for board and lodge until Saturday. If the owner's not there, wait for him. Show this to him and him only. Are you listening, Hannah?"

"Yes, yes I am, but I don't understand," she cried.

"It's important, Hannah. No one else must know you have any connection to me. Understand? You would be in danger if certain people thought you had a link to me. They would use you to get to me," he continued.

"Daniel, you're scaring me now. What do you mean? How will I be in danger?" She was almost shouting.

"Look, just do as I ask. If anyone asks you anything, don't mention me at all. Just say you are heading to Kingsmead to visit an aunt, that's it, no more. Not even the owner needs to know, though he won't ask any questions. Understand?" Daniel finished talking.

She spoke again, more calmly now. "No, I don't understand but I will do as you ask. I have no choice."

"We all have choices, Hannah, but it's how we live with the consequences that is important."

Hurrying the horse on, she realised the conversation was over. By the time they reached Dealham, the rain had turned into a drizzle.

"Pack everything of yours. Leave nothing behind," he ordered her.

She didn't speak. She just fastened the ribbons of her bonnet under her chin. Her shawl was tightly knotted around her shoulders. Getting down from the cart, her voice was quivering as she spoke, "I won't see you again, will I?"

"Of course you will. I'll meet you here early Saturday morning just as the sun rises. I know someone who will buy Bobby but you won't get his full value. If anything changes, I will get a message to you. I promised to take you to Kingsmead and I will," Daniel retorted. "Now go before you get soaked."

Walking down the road, she held herself upright, shoulders back, head up, in spite of the rain. She wasn't cowed but had a determination about her. She didn't turn back to look at him but walked at a fair pace until out of sight.

CHAPTER FIVE
DANIEL'S STORY

Turning the cart around, Daniel thought that their lives hadn't been too different. He hadn't been sold into a marriage but he had cared for himself from a young age. He wasn't proud of it but he had killed a man to protect another and, like Hannah, it had changed his life forever.

He didn't want to become maudlin. His early childhood had been happy, one of six children. His parents were not rich by any means but made a living none the less working a tithe farm. He smiled as he remembered the first time he ate too many unripe apples, spending almost a week in bed with stomach cramps. His brothers and sisters all went to school but he preferred being outside, helping his father. What his life would have been like if his father had not died in an accident when Daniel was twelve, he didn't know. Within days of the funeral, his mother was given notice to move out of the farm. She had hugged him tightly and sat stroking his hair gently while she tried to hold back her tears as she explained that he would be going to live with his Uncle Joseph and Aunt Emma near Betton. He didn't know where that was. He had only just met his father's brother at the funeral and had never met his aunt.

His mother went on to explain that he would be leaving with his uncle that day and he was to be a brave boy. She would be taking the three younger children to live with her parents in Swallham but they couldn't take in anymore. It was very kind of his uncle, she said, to take him into the family.

Daniel had wanted to go with his older brother to work on a farm in the next village, but that wasn't an option as they couldn't afford to pay for another farmhand. His older sister was already in service at a large hall several miles away.

He didn't cry when the younger children cried, nor did he raise his head or wave as his uncle's cart took him from the only home he had known. His mother had promised to write to him regularly but he knew he would have difficulty reading her letter or penning a reply. He had never taken to sitting in a classroom, thought it was a waste of time. It didn't teach him how to milk a cow or help a sow give birth. His father had taught him that.

Though he had wanted to jump off the cart and run away, he hadn't. He'd sat stock still. It was probably the death of his father or the shock of his mother giving him away that turned him into a brooding, almost surly, young man. Whatever his guardians asked him to do he did, with attitude, which didn't endear him to them or their two daughters. His Uncle Joseph was a marshman, plying his trade along the river Waveton to Southwood and beyond. It was soon clear to Daniel that he was expected to work on the river too. The work was hard but he thought it must be well paid as his aunt and cousins were always buying new hats and ribbons. There was plenty of food on the table and his uncle had money in his pocket for ale. His paternal grandfather had rented the clinker-built wherry, though his uncle had bought it when he took over.

Daniel learnt a lot about wherrys but he never fell in love with the water. He learnt that the fore and aft rig was carried on a large mast which was finely counterbalanced at the heel to allow easy lowering but Daniel didn't think so in those early days as he hauled the sail up or down. Within a year of living with his aunt and uncle, he had grown tall, his arms tanned and muscled. By the time he was fifteen, he looked every inch a man yet his face had a sallow tinge. It surprised him how much he had changed as he had always been outside on the farm.

His uncle was a strict disciplinarian so Daniel learned things the hard way. When he first went off as a mate to his uncle, he had no idea about the whys and wherefores of sail. He still had weal mark scars on his back from the rigging. He could feel the lump on the back of his head where the beam had swung round lifting him off his feet and knocking him out. His uncle thought he was dead but laughed until he cried as Daniel came to. His head hurt for days, though he got little sympathy from the rest of the family who also laughed loudly as his uncle regaled them with the story over dinner.

The need to survive drove him on. He wanted to show everyone he could manage on his own. Once he met some people when they travelled as far as Northton who offered to take him on but he wanted to bide his time. He wanted to learn all he could before becoming his own boss.

The wherrymen had a special wheelbarrow which was made from wood strengthened with iron bands. Daniel's hands soon blistered and bled as he pushed the barrow up the planks onto dry land. At first, the boat was filled with stone to build new houses, later with coal to heat the same houses. There were certain items he was not allowed to unload. A cart would turn up on the tow path, usually at dusk. His uncle would unload the items himself while Daniel was sent off to clean the deck or the planks around the wherry.

He was never paid a wage. He got board and lodge as well as a few clothes. His aunt said he didn't need a wage. He became smart. He knew if he was to get away, he would need money. His uncle would regularly send him as a runner to the nearest mill if the Customs and Excise men were about. He was quick and surefooted, reaching the windmills at the first sign of trouble. If there was a wind, he would climb onto the sail and his weight would be a counterbalance to stop the sails turning. The marshman would halt the sails in the shape of a Saint Andrew diagonal cross, then wait until the next windmill had stopped their sails in the same position. They would then be re-started, thwarting the men looking for smuggled items.

For this, Daniel would sometimes be paid a penny, or even a three penny piece, which he would hide, ready for a life of his own.

He also stole money from his uncle but only what he thought he was due. His uncle would often return from various trips in a drunken state and Daniel would keep a penny or tuppence. He once took a sixpence but his uncle had a vague recollection of having one, hunting around for it while shouting profanities at Daniel who thought it best to say nothing.

Soon Daniel began undercutting his uncle whilst selling contraband barrels of ale. When the threat of the Excise men became too close for comfort, the barrels would be removed from the wherry and placed amongst the reeds, sunk until the threat was over. Occasionally one would lose its moorings, rolling into deeper water, or so his uncle thought. Daniel soon had a nice collection of coins. Another year and he would be able to strike out on his own.

However, his decision was to be made much sooner than he anticipated. One night, he and his uncle had only travelled half a day upstream from home when they tied up the wherry for the night. His uncle said he had business to attend to and disappeared into the town and the local hostelry.

As it was a clear warm night, Daniel took himself off into the woods and the direction of old Albarn Tamblyn's cottage where he knew he would be made welcome. They often talked when Albarn ferried goods into the villages with an old cart and an even older horse named Bess. Albarn was getting old, his bones ached and he didn't get visitors often so he was pleased to have Daniel's company as he sat on an old chair outside the wooden hut, smoking his pipe.

As it started to get dark, Daniel took his leave of the kindly old man. His eyes adjusted to the darkness of the woods as he walked at a good pace toward the river. The stars were out by the time Daniel headed back toward the wherry. He wanted to be in his bunk and asleep before his uncle got back.

Hearing raised voices, he slowed his pace keeping to the treeline so he wouldn't be noticed as the moon lit up the rough track. His uncle was shouting and staggering toward a man who was also shouting but the man was standing perfectly still with his back to Daniel. As the man raised his arm, Daniel saw a crop in his hand which struck his uncle about the head and shoulders as he fell to the ground. The man kicked out at Daniel's uncle before jumping on his legs. Daniel heard a sharp crack.

Within seconds, he had managed to reach the wherry without

being seen, picked up the shovel and swung it at the man, almost knocking his head from his shoulders. Dropping like a stone on top of his uncle, the man was dead, he was sure of it.

His uncle screaming brought Daniel to his senses. Rolling the man onto his back, he felt his heart but there was nothing.

"Roll him into the river, boy," his uncle yelled, in between groaning.

Grabbing the man under his arms, Daniel pulled him to the river bank. He didn't know to this day why he did it but he checked the man's pockets. A small bag of money and a customs card with his name on it, Edward Willows, Kingsmead, was all he could make out with his poor reading skills. Daniel replaced the card and left the gold ring on the dead man's finger. Poor sod's got a wife, he thought, but he kept hold of the money. Pushing the body with his boot, he watched as it splashed before rolling and sinking under the water.

Daniel walked over to his uncle who was whimpering. He looked down at this pathetic man. One of his legs was quite badly twisted. Blood was all over his face and hands where he had tried to protect himself.

"Get me up, boy. Get me onto the boat," his uncle snarled.

"Wait!" Daniel replied, picking up the shovel before returning to the boat. He went down into the cabin, picking up his uncle's straw mattress and blanket. He lay them on the deck at the aft, before returning to his uncle who was now screaming like a banshee.

"Shut up, shut up or you'll have the whole village here," Daniel said, shoving a stick into his uncle's mouth to stem the noise. Kneeling down, he grabbed the twisted leg, straightening it next to the other before binding them together with rags. His uncle screamed and gurgled before becoming silent. Heaving his uncle up under his arms, Daniel staggered to the boat, laying him on his back on the mattress before throwing the blanket over him.

Then grabbing the bucket, he swung it into the river on the opposite side to where he had rolled Mr Willow's body. He threw the water onto the grass where his uncle's blood lay in a dark pool, hoping it would have disappeared by morning.

Untying the ropes, Daniel pushed the fore of the wherry into the middle of the river. After several attempts, he turned it so it would float downstream. This was a lazy yawning stretch of the river so they plodded downstream very slowly. There was no wind for the sail. He didn't want to use the pole and draw attention to themselves. Sitting at the aft, sticking to the middle of the river, he watched as dawn rose over the trees.

His uncle groaned but remained unconscious all night. It gave Daniel time to formulate a plan. He opened the bag of money and found twenty shillings, a fortune to him. It pained him to think how he had got it. The poor man didn't deserve to die. His uncle had a lot to answer for, selling and smuggling contraband.

The family were very surprised to see him so early in the morning. His aunt began weeping when she saw the state of her husband who was now whimpering on a sofa in the parlour. Daniel sent his cousins off to get a doctor and asked his aunt to go into the kitchen to arrange tea.

Telling his uncle he was leaving was much easier than he thought. To be fair, Daniel made it clear that he was to say that he had fallen onto the boat when drunk, breaking his leg. Daniel had seen enough of what went on and wanted to go his own way. Should his uncle mention to anyone what had happened, he would blow the whistle on his games, even naming names, making sure someone would do for him.

With that, he went up to his sparse room, pulling what spare clothing he had into the middle of his blankets before knotting them in the centre. The blankets were sent with him from his mother and they were all he had of his family.

Then taking his money from the wherry, without looking back at his now hysterical aunt, he set off in the direction of Albarn Tamblyn's home.

CHAPTER SIX
THE GREEN MAN

Hannah heard the horse and cart turn around but didn't want to watch them go. Her tears mixed with the large raindrops now beginning to fall. Her head remained held high, striding forward as though she knew where she was going. Once she thought they were out of sight, she looked back but he was gone. The lights of Dealham beckoned her onwards, into the market square which was bigger than she had imagined.

The Green Man was to the left hand side of the square. The main entrance had double doors with a single light overhead. She was afraid to go into a public bar on her own so continued to the left and down a small pathway between buildings. Not finding another entrance, she returned to the front of the building intending to try the other side. Just as she was about to walk past the doors, they opened and a man staggered out. She tried to hurry past, but he grabbed her. The stale smell of ale made her want to retch. Throwing all her weight behind her bundle, she almost managed to knock him off his feet, only he fell onto her. Screaming at him, she tried to pull further away but his weight pushed them both to the ground. The commotion brought people out into the street. An arm helped her up as she tried to shake it off.

"The lass looks as though she could do with a drink," someone said as she was led into the bar and shown to a seat at a table.

A glass of brandy was placed in front of her which she gulped in one go, screwing up her face as she swallowed. It could have been the brandy, the warm room, or even the stench of stale ale, but the last thing she remembered was the sound of laughter as she slid to the floor.

Her eyes fluttered open before closing tightly against the light. She was trying to think where she was. Opening them again, she spotted her shawl and bonnet on the chair opposite an unlit fire grate. Her blanket bundle was on the floor beside them. Behind her head was a soft pillow and a blanket covered her legs. Oh what an entrance, she thought, finally remembering where she was. Moving the blanket to attempt to rise, a movement from beside the window startled her.

"There you are, my beauty, gave us a right scare, make no mistake. Now you stay where you are and I'll get the mister to bring you a nice cup of tea." Without waiting for a reply, the stout lady whose hair was knotted tightly at the top of her head went out of the open door. She shouted, "James, James, the lass is awake. Fetch her up a drink," before marching down the stairs.

Closing her eyes, Hannah fell back into sleep, only to wake sharply when she heard the scraping of a chair on the polished wooden floor. The man who had helped her into the bar was sitting on the chair.

"Now then lass, can we get a message to someone to come and fetch you? You've had a bad fall but I don't think anything's broken." His voice was gentle, belaying his bulky frame.

"No, no one. Are you the landlord?" she asked, looking directly at him.

"Aye I am, for my sins, lass."

Hannah rummaged in her dress pocket for the cord necklace Daniel had given her.

"He said to show you this and ask for bed and board until early Saturday morning. Will that be alright, Mister...? Sorry, I don't know your name."

"Just call me James, lass. Any friend of Daniel's is welcome here, but let's just say you are looking for work, no need to tell my ma anything else, alright?" He smiled at her. "The lady is my mother, not much of a lady but her bark's worse than her bite." He laughed at his own joke. "She could do with some help in the kitchen, but not tonight, though, eh? You've had a nasty shock."

She was about to speak but he held up his hand. "Now we'll say no more. You drink your tea. I'll speak to ma and light a fire in one of the guest rooms along the landing."

With that, he left her to take in her surroundings. Everything in the room was old and shabby, careworn but highly polished. Even the hearth was free from ash but though the fire was set, it wasn't lit. Maybe it wasn't used much if they were in the bar all day, she thought. Antimacassars were on every arm and back of chairs, hand embroidered by the look of it. Little lace doilies sat on side tables.

Replacing the necklace in her pocket, she felt for the gun and wedding ring before remembering she had placed them in the middle of her bundle. She was about to get up when the door opened and the woman pushed it with her large rear, a tray in her hand.

"Right missy, our James tells me you are staying for a few days to help me in the kitchen. I've been asking for help for months but he won't put his hand in his pocket."

"I hope I can be of help. I'll try my best. The name's Hannah," she said, trying to stand up.

"No, you don't. Have my guts for garters he would. My lad said tomorrow so tomorrow it is. My name's Primrose, Primmy, I get. Father liked his garden so called us girls after flowers. Sisters are Daisy, Violet, Poppy, Rose and me. Now eat your dinner then one of us will show you to your room," and she strode out of the room and back down the stairs.

Staring at the door, Hannah wanted to laugh and cry at the same time. Primmy was funny; her voice was gruff but she obviously thought the world of her son. Hannah wanted to cry at the kindness of Daniel's friends yet again. As with Mrs Whisker, they didn't comment, were simply willing to help Daniel without question. How she had wished she had had friends to turn to but this hadn't been allowed when she was a child and certainly not when she married.

Later, she sat in bed watching the flames flicker as the coals cooled. She sipped at the cup of hot milk which was laced with more brandy. It would help her sleep, they said, soothe her bones after her fall. This time, she quite enjoyed the warm feeling. Her baby kicked, much to her relief, and hands resting on her stomach, she fell into a deep sleep.

The following morning, Hannah put on a brave face as she entered the kitchen. Her back and shoulders felt stiff, and her legs were painful but she didn't want to let it show.

Primmy was in her element having someone to talk to. She had a list of tasks for Hannah to perform. Her voice went on and on. Wash the tankards and glasses not once but twice, first in the soapy water then rinse in clear water. Once they are clean, leave them to drain while wiping down the tables and bar top. Hannah couldn't get a word in, so she just nodded as Primmy continued. Chairs onto tables, sweep then wash the floor. Brush, mop and bucket in the yard along with the cold water tap.

Her head was spinning as she started gathering up the beer tankards, the yeasty smell making her feel queasy. She would never get used to it. Moving quickly to try and wash the beer fumes away, she found herself humming while she worked.

When James came up from the cellar, he roared with laughter. "I haven't seen the place looking so clean for a long time. I know Ma finds it hard so you're a godsend, lass. Come and sit with us at the table while we eat breakfast," he said, taking the mop out of her hand.

Primmy started talking as soon as they entered the kitchen. James must have warned his mother not to ask questions so at least Hannah didn't have to tell any lies.

Later, Hannah sang while mopping the stairs to the living quarters when two dogs rushed up to her, almost knocking her off her feet and the mop out of her hand. Laddie and Spot danced round her legs, tails wagging. Stepping onto the still damp floor, she sat on the stairs hugging the dogs to her.

Voices rang out from the yard and both dogs ran in front of her but she stopped when she heard Daniel speak. "She's nothing to me, James. I'm taking her to Kingsmead, that's all."

"Well, Ma's took a shine to her. She's willing to work. She could do worse than stay here," James responded.

"Aw, this is no place for a child."

"She's not a child though, is she?" James snapped.

"No, she's having a baby, that's what I'm saying. Don't look at me like that, James. It's nothing to do with me. Like I said, I promised to take her to Kingsmead and I will. Then that's it!" Daniel must have moved away as his voice grew more distant.

Scurrying back to the half-mopped stairs, Hannah was upset and hurt, really hurt. Deep down she knew she meant nothing to him, why would she? But he had been kind, now his voice sounded almost brutal. Men, she thought, they are all the same… heartless. Picking up the mop, she cleaned the stairs with an anger she didn't know she had in her. Her chores were finished in silence. She didn't feel like singing anymore.

Hannah assumed James had told his mother she was pregnant though neither of them asked her any questions. She wasn't going to break the silence, Primmy would do that. They ate their evening meal then James left to open the bar while she took the bowls to the sink.

It was then that Primmy spoke. "We'll be busy tomorrow as the market is in the square. You will be expected to help wherever you are needed."

"That's fine, Primmy. I'll do whatever I can." She suddenly felt exhausted and didn't want to go into the bar but Primmy had other ideas.

"Take these into the side room and set the tables," she said, passing the tablecloths, mats and cutlery. "The tables by the windows are two settings, the other tables set for four then come back for the crockery."

Going through the bar, Hannah was pleased to see only a few men at a table playing dominoes. The pristine white tablecloths all had embroidered flowers circled in the middle with bluebells, daffodils or tulips. Each corner had a small spray of flowers of similar colours with green ivy running along the hem. Cups, saucers, matching small plates and cutlery were all set out. The tables held cards with the same numbers as the trays so that the teapot, hot water jug, sugar bowl and milk jug all matched the table settings. Plain, large white plates were sitting on the tables with small doilies which had been crocheted in white around the edge. Small vases of flowers finished the table decoration.

Primmy explained that on market days, they opened the side door for ladies to come in for lunch or just a cup of tea. By using the side door, they would not have to go through the bar.

Hannah had to wear a long white apron and mob cap, though her hair kept springing out from all sides, making Primmy shout at her for being untidy. The shouting gave slight relief from the one sided conversation which had started first thing that morning. Large joints of ham and beef had been roasted the day before. Hannah was attempting to slice it as thinly as she could while Primmy was making pastry for scones and tarts. Small fancies were on a tray cooling whilst waiting to be iced.

Hannah watched intently as the lunch began to take shape. Primmy told her that it was all the fashion in London society. Women would meet for luncheon while in town. She had spoken to James about turning the small room into a tea house on market days. He had agreed. Smiling, Hannah thought no one would dare disagree with Primmy, not even her son. She was a formidable character though they obviously thought a lot about each other. Primmy had thought that the farmers' wives might frequent the tea house whilst waiting for their husbands to finish at the auction. It had taken off. Now ladies' maids, vicars' wives and small groups of young ladies waiting for their fathers had become regulars. For a set price, they received dainty sandwiches, a scone with homemade jam and cream, cheese tart and a few fancies with as much tea as they could drink. The meat, milk, cream and cheese were all sourced locally, brought to the inn by the farmers.

From mid-morning, Hannah carried trays of tea as well as plates of food from the kitchen and into the tea room, which was full from the opening of the door. She had to remember to bob her knee each time she left a table. As quickly as she cleared a table, another group of women sat down. Primmy was like a dervish, washing up, piling plates high, making fresh pots of tea as soon as the empty pot was brought back. James was busy all day too, serving drinks in the bar. Hannah assumed he was washing his own mugs and glasses.

The tray was heavy but she did manage to push the door open by entering the room backwards. Placing the tray on a small side table, she managed to squeeze in between the tables without dropping anything. It would have been wonderful to stop and listen to the conversations or look at the clothing but she was too busy. Occasionally she noticed a nice brooch, lace gloves or shoes with small buttons to fasten them. It made her feel very dowdy. Her grey dress was stained along the hemline while her boots needed a good polish. At least her hands and fingernails were clean even if they were still rough.

By the time she closed the door on the last of the ladies, her feet and back were throbbing with pain. She would have loved to have taken her boots off and rubbed her aching feet but instead she pulled out a chair and sat down at one of the tables. Taking off her cap, she put her head in her hands. This was how Primmy found her some time later.

"Eh lass, you're dead on your feet. Give me a hand to clear the tables then we'll have a bite to eat." Primmy took Hannah's arm to help her up.

Primmy didn't speak as she passed her a cup of hot tea and a plate of sandwiches and cake left over from lunch. Hannah could hardly lift her hand to her mouth.

"You did well today, lass. The ladies left plenty of tips." Primmy counted out some money. "There you are. That will help you on your way."

Looking at the coins, there was at least two shillings and sixpence, a fortune she was desperate for but she couldn't take it. They had housed her for the last five days for nothing. Yes, she had worked really hard but she hadn't expected any payment.

"Thank you, Primmy, but I really couldn't take it when you have been so kind."

"Nonsense, lass, it's not my money. You've worked for it. The women left it for you. Now put it in your pocket, we'll say no more about it."

Hannah could feel the tears prickle her eyes. It had to stop. This was her life and the consequence of what she had done to her husband. Her old life seemed years rather than weeks ago, and she was amazed how easily she had left it behind. If she could only get a message to her mother, she could have coped.

Primmy brought her back to the present when she said, "Let's get this washing up sorted out. While it's drying, we need to move the tables, we've a funeral in that room tomorrow."

The rest of the evening passed in a blur. The only time she spoke to James was when Primmy took over in the bar and he came into the kitchen for his evening meal.

"I don't know how Primmy manages on her own," Hannah said, trying to make conversation.

"We've had girls here before but they didn't take to Ma, or her to them. Most didn't want to live in a pub. They would rather go into service in the big houses where they have more company," he responded.

"Perhaps you should find yourself a wife," she said, immediately regretting saying it and wishing she could have taken it back.

She went red and hot when he replied, "Is that an offer, Hannah? Ma's taken quite a shine to you."

The thought of being married to anyone made her gasp, apart from which she didn't know if her husband was actually dead.

"It's alright, lass, I know I'm not everyone's cup of tea and it would be a brave woman who would share a kitchen with Ma."

"No, no, James, it's not that. You have both been really kind to me and under different circumstances, I would have stayed though I don't ever want to marry anyone. My aunt is expecting me in Kingsmead, I can't let her down. I'm sorry."

James patted her arm as he left the room, neither had mentioned the large problem of her baby.

The day had been pandemonium and she was exhausted but she cleared away what she could as Primmy returned. "Come on, girl, take that jug of hot water up to bed with you. You're done in."

Nodding, Hannah left the room, walking slowly up the stairs, struggling to put one foot in front of the other.

Someone had lit a fire in her room, making a warm soft glow. After washing herself, even though she just wanted to collapse into bed, she placed the bowl on the floor by the fire. Sitting in her nightgown, the one Mrs Whisker had given her, she placed her feet into the warm water as her eyelids began to droop. She wanted to sleep, wishing she had put her blanket around her shoulders. Forcing herself to get up, she dried her feet before rinsing her underwear in the now tepid water. She hung the clothes on the back of a chair close to the fire to dry before going to bed. Snuggling under the covers, she was asleep before her head touched the pillow.

The following morning, her mind was alert though her body still ached all over. She had bruises from the fall which, luckily, were hidden. Her feet complained as soon as she fastened her shoes. It surprised her how tired she felt as she had worked hard from morning till night from being a child. It must be the baby, she thought, as she hadn't any experience of that.

Primmy and James were already in the kitchen and when she got down the stairs, a plate of food was placed in front of her.

"One more day of being bossed around by Ma. Are you ready for it?" James laughed.

"I certainly am. Whatever you throw at me, I can deal with," she responded, keeping her voice light.

James went off to the cellar to check on the barrels while Primmy gave her the orders for the day.

While she was cleaning the table in the bar, the butcher came in with a box of pork pies. He seemed a pleasant man who passed the time of day with her. She didn't know where his shop was, she hadn't stepped outside since the night she arrived but he had certainly heard about her. He told her that word travels fast in Dealham where everyone knows everyone's business. Primmy told him to stop his slaver as he was stopping the work.

"I love it when you speak to me like that," he laughed at Primmy. "When are you going to marry me?"

She shooed him out as she waved a cloth at him, both laughing.

Shortly afterwards, a baker's lad came in. He blushed with embarrassment when Hannah spoke to him.

That day, she had been given a black apron and mob cap. Primmy had already sent her off to the water tap in the yard to dampen her hair to keep it in place. It was an easier day than yesterday. Once the large pan of soup, bread, ham, cheese and pork pies had been placed on the table, she left James to serve the drinks for the men. Primmy told her it was an estate manager who had died in an accident. He had been thrown from his horse, breaking his neck before he caught a fever and died. A large number of men had attended the funeral but instead of having a feast at his widow's, they were coming to the inn. The ladies would adjourn to the home.

The bar became very raucous as the men started drinking, wandering between the room and bar. Taking a tray of fresh plates, bread and ham, Hannah stopped at the buffet table. As she was moving the dirty plates onto the tray, a man grabbed her arm. "Girl, I know you. Where have I seen your pretty face before?"

Pulling her arm away and almost knocking the plates to the floor, she replied, "No, I don't think so, sir," keeping her head down so he couldn't see the fear in her eyes. She tried to side step him but he grasped her chin tightly in his hand, turning her toward him, lifting her head so he could see her more clearly.

Swaying toward her, she thought he was going to kiss her. None of the other men took any notice so she kicked him hard on the shins, screaming loudly, "Get your hands off me, leave me alone!" before running into the kitchen where she sobbed loudly.

"What's going on?" Primmy snapped. "What's wrong with you? You're shaking."

She couldn't speak, she couldn't catch her breath. That man was drunk but what if he did know her, what if he knew her husband. Running into the yard, she was sick. What if he remembered where she was from? Taking the cap off, she sluiced her face under the tap before returning to the kitchen.

"Sit down, lass. Sit down before you fall down. What's wrong with you?" Primmy looked at her concerned.

Before she could answer, there was a commotion then laughter in the bar as James came into the kitchen. "What's all this, staff attacking one of my valued customers?"

"Serves him right," Hannah responded defiantly, "he grabbed me."

"You've certainly livened up the wake. He says he knows you, is that true?"

"No, he doesn't know me!" she cried.

Going back to the bar, James shouted to her, "You can take your things and leave tomorrow, got that?" and he winked at her.

Primmy sat down. "Eh lass, I don't know what's going on in that head of yours. Something's not right, mark my words. I don't suppose you are going to share it with me, are you?"

Hannah shook her head slowly. She had nothing to say.

All too soon, she was packing her bundle ready for the early start the following morning. She placed her money in the cloth purse with her wedding ring and pistol for safety. What she was going to do with them she didn't know, but she felt she might need them at some point in her life. Earlier in the evening, she had thanked them both for their kindness toward her which she would never forget. Primmy finally mentioned her pregnancy, saying that under different circumstances she would have liked her to stay but a pregnant worker would bring the place into disrepute. James stood by her side, saying nothing, but he patted her on the shoulder as he left the room.

She had a fitful sleep that night afraid that Daniel wouldn't be waiting for her tomorrow. He had promised. He had said he would take her all the way to Kingsmead. What she would do there she didn't know.

It was still black outside as she hugged both Primmy and James.

"Take care of yourself, lass. If you ever pass this way, you'll be welcome," they both said in their own way. Pushing a package into her hand, they walked her to the door.

"Thank you again, both of you," Hannah said. "I'll never forget it."

With that, she turned, walking across the market square, back the way she had walked a few days earlier.

CHAPTER SEVEN
THE JOURNEY WEST

With each step, she prayed that Daniel would be there to meet her. Walking back to the crossroads in the dark, she kept her head down so as not to fall in the ruts the wagons had made in the dirt. Hearing horses' hooves, she looked down the track, seeing Pinto striding toward her. She smiled. She wanted to pick up her skirt and run toward him. It was silly but when she was with Daniel, she felt safe. It didn't matter about those things he had said about her, he was here keeping his promise to take her further away.

Pulling at the reins for the horse to stop, he jumped down in almost the same move. The dogs were certainly happy to see her as Daniel placed her bundle into the cart. Helping her up, he spoke for the first time. "Did you enjoy your stay at the Green Man? Did Primmy talk your ears off?"

"She certainly is a character but she works really hard. I'm not sure how they managed when they were busy," she laughed.

Daniel told her that he had managed to sell Bobby to a drover who also took a few horses to sell at auctions further west. He hadn't got market price for him but no questions were asked. Taking the fifteen shillings, she thanked him before putting them in her dress pocket for now. Later she would transfer the money to her purse.

They continued the general chatter as the dark morning turned into a light autumn day. The billowing clouds floated across a pale blue sky like the frayed hem of a skirt, all ragged at the edges. Although she was worried what would happen to her when they reached Kingsmead, she was enjoying the fresh air as well as Daniel's company. He seemed less sullen and in a good frame of mind. She thought this might be a good time to ask how he had become a traveller and she listened while he gave her a monologue of his life.

He told her about his childhood, cut short when his father died. How he lived with his uncle and aunt. He continued to tell her how he ended up living in the forest with Albarn Tamblyn who taught him how to train Pinto when he bought him as an untrained colt.

"We'd sit outside the cabin," he said, "and Mr Tamblyn would show me how to gain the trust of the horse. We extended the lean to, making it dry so it could be used as a stable for both horses. One wall backed onto the cabin where the chimney made the stable warmer. We used both horses to drag large felled trees to weatherproof the other walls and roof. I would chop wood and kindling in the evening so that the fire could remain on at all times. Having me there seemed to give Mr Tamblyn a new lease of life." He seemed almost wistful. "We were inseparable," he said. "For the first time in years, I was happy. We would travel together delivering goods from the wherrys to the villages, or special deliveries under the cover of darkness."

He was quiet for a while then added, "My uncle never recovered from an accident. I heard that later on my travels. And one of my cousins was married off to a widowed butcher."

He laughed loudly at that point and Hannah joined in although she didn't know why.

"Mr Tamblyn struggled during the winter months with just Bess," he went on, "so I put Pinto into the shafts. I did the trading on my own but I always handed the money over to Mr Tamblyn who shared it equally. We trusted each other implicitly. I would not have dreamed of making any money on the side."

"What happened?" Hannah said, wondering why Daniel was alone.

"Mr Tamblyn caught a chill the second winter and never recovered," he said. "It felt as if I had lost a father all over again. In respect to Albarn Tamblyn, I paid for his funeral. It was surprising how many people attended the church, many men patting me on the back like a son. They hoped I would continue the business of moving the smuggled contraband around the country."

Hannah gasped when she heard this, no wonder he didn't want her to be associated with him. She wanted to ask questions but was afraid he would clam up so she sat back whilst he continued.

"I still visit Mr Tamblyn's grave when I am in the area," he said. "I spent the remainder of the winter and spring building this caravan so I could be more comfortable and ply my trade further afield. These days I spend the worst of the winter and Christmas with my sister and her family who had remained in our grandparents' home when my mother died."

"Is that the sister who sent the waistcoats to Mrs Whisker?" she asked.

"Yes, Emily, she is always making something. I think she starts her Christmas knitting in January. I hope I get a jumper this year," he continued.

"It must be nice to be able to knit and sew," Hannah responded. "I can sew straight edges but that's about it."

The next few days passed pleasantly as they travelled at a good pace toward Kingsmead. The nights were cooling down so they all shared the tiny caravan space. Daniel let her have the narrow bed while he spent the night fighting for space with the dogs on the floor.

It was mid-morning on the Wednesday when they reached the outskirts of Kingsmead. Hannah's stomach was churning. She felt sick. It wasn't anything to do with her baby or the travelling; she was frightened. She knew she would soon be on her own with no one to look out for her.

Clearing her throat, she put her hand on Daniel's arm. "I want to thank you so much for all the kindness and care you have shown me. I would never have made it on my own. I realise that now." She started to cry.

"Hey, come on, Hannah, your adventure isn't over yet. I'm not promising anything but I have a friend in Kingsmead who might need help. Let me see what I can come up with." He patted her hand as she nodded.

Wiping her eyes with her hands, she couldn't speak. She was certain she would be dead, or even on trial for murder if she hadn't met Daniel. The tears rolled down her cheeks unabated now. She couldn't look at him. Although she knew that this was coming, that she would be alone again, she had felt safe with Daniel. The tears flowed but she knew she had to move on. Pulling herself together, she wiped away the tears and gave him a smile.

As they headed onward, she saw in the distance what looked like a large castle with turrets and two windows looking in the direction they had travelled. She saw lots of people walking through smaller arches at either side of a large arch which the cart went through. The people looked dirty, wearing rags, whilst many of the children didn't have any boots. They sat in the archway sheltering from the cold. They looked pitiful, she thought, as they begged for money from the carts.

Daniel led Pinto into a market square similar to the one the Green Man was in, though much larger. Hannah's eyes lit up when she saw the architecture of the buildings on all sides. She would have loved to wander round, or just watch people going about their everyday business but Pinto continued down a narrow lane which had shops on either side before turning into an even narrower back lane.

Eventually Daniel pulled the horse to a stop before jumping down and opening a large wooden gate. He led the horse and cart into a square yard where there was just enough room for both. Helping Hannah down, he said, "Look, we will go through the back door but wait in the lobby while I speak to the lady of the house."

Hannah nodded, holding her blanket in front of her. She followed Daniel into the small square lobby and waited as he went on. Suddenly she heard a woman's voice.

"Daniel, oh Daniel, I wasn't expecting you before tomorrow. Oh, it's so good to see you. I have missed you so much."

Hannah heard him reply, "Adele, you look lovely, as usual. How are you? Mrs Willows still the same?"

It went quiet for a short while and Hannah assumed they were hugging or kissing. She wasn't expecting that, but then why not? Daniel had never mentioned a sweetheart but he was a presentable young man even if he was a traveller. It was tempting to move closer to the small gap in the door to see what the lady looked like but she was afraid she would be seen. Instead, she remained standing like a statue, hardly daring to breathe.

"Mother is getting worse, she's had me up and down the stairs till I've met myself coming back. I can't work in the shop and tend to her. I'm worn out. Her dropsy is getting worse because she won't get out of bed. I'm struggling to lift her. Oh listen to me, Daniel. I am so glad you are here. I don't know how much more I can take. I want to be married, Daniel, I want to be your wife."

There was silence again before Daniel spoke. "I know, I know, but Mrs Willows won't give her consent. We can wait however long it takes. Now I may have a solution to your problem. On my travels I met a young lady who is looking for work. She could deal with Mrs Willows, cook and clean. What do you say, Adele?"

Adele sounded angry. "What's this? You want me to take one of your women into my home? Never, Daniel, never!"

"What are you talking about? She's nothing to do with me. I told you, she was on the road, pregnant with nowhere to go."

"So now you are telling me she is pregnant and you just managed to come across her. Give me some credit, Daniel, I'm not stupid. How convenient that would be for you to have us both under the same roof?" Adele's voice rose higher. "She's not coming here, I might be desperate but I won't be made a cuckold of. You know what mother would say if she knew!"

Hannah heard a slap. She'd heard enough. She turned and headed out of the door and into the yard.

Daniel tried to placate Adele by talking softly to her. "Listen to me, her name is Hannah, she's only a girl. Her husband's dead and she's pregnant. You don't know how many people I see on the road, it's awful, Adele." He took her hand thinking he couldn't say Hannah had murdered her husband, he was sure she would never speak of it. "I would never have mentioned it but I can see how you're fixed. Your mother will outlive you if you continue like this." He put his hand on her neck pulling her close to him. It disclosed a large birthmark running from her ear, down her throat and neck. Without this, he would never have stood a chance to court her. He knew that men would be lining up for her hand but superstition that she was somehow tainted stopped them. She had strawberry blonde hair, the bluest eyes he had ever seen. Her skin was as white as alabaster with just the lightest flush to her cheeks. She was beautiful make no mistake. But then God had put this mark on her to stop her becoming vain.

Holding her to him, he remembered the first time he had seen her. It was almost six years ago when he was sharpening knives in the market and she passed him with her mother. They were both dressed from head to toe in black, in mourning. He asked about them in the hostelry while supping ale later that evening. Mrs Willows and Miss Adele, he was told, had continued to wear black long after the respectable time. Just like good old Queen Victoria, the men laughed. The mother thought she was a cut above. Poor Adele was afflicted with a birth mark, they continued. Mr Willows had been an excise man who had drowned doing official business so they received a small pension. Adele was good at sewing, making gowns and bonnets in the parlour of their home for anyone who would buy them.

Daniel went outside and was violently sick. He blamed too much ale but he knew this was the family of the man he had murdered all those years ago. It had come back to haunt him, he knew he would have to do something to help them if he could without anyone knowing what he had done.

It happened sooner than he thought, bumping into them quite literally the following day. He turned a corner, walking into them, knocking some packages out of Adele's hands. Picking them up, he carried them back to their house. From then on, he always spoke to them. Though Adele was painfully shy, he persevered. They saw each other several times while he was at the market but as he moved on it could be months before he saw her again.

Braving a rebuff, he asked Mrs Willows if they could walk later in the afternoon. Adele begged her to say yes. Putting on his better clothes, the three of them walked through the park where he offered to take them for tea which was a strained affair. Their relationship stuttered and struggled as Daniel came and went, but he knew that even with the guilt of her father's death, he loved Adele. But Mrs Willows' dislike of him worked to his advantage as he wasn't ready to settle in one place just yet.

Now Adele was a young woman who had stepped out of the black and into soft colours, dresses with high collars which only enhanced her beauty. Mrs Willows remained in black which did nothing to endear her to anyone. To Daniel, she looked like the devil herself when she set eyes on him.

However in some ways, he had become settled as the shop with rooms above where they now lived belonged to him. He had purchased it at least three years ago after spotting Adele rushing through the market square alone. Following her, he stood waiting until she stepped from the doctors, where he stopped her.

"Adele, my love, what's wrong? Has something happened to Mrs Willows?" He took her arm which wasn't seemly but he didn't think.

"Oh Daniel, I'm glad to see you, I really am. Mother's had a turn, we've had bad news and she has collapsed. I must get back," she replied, walking quickly.

"Let me walk with you and you can tell me all about it."

"We've been given notice to move out of our home. A new excise family need it and we have nowhere to go. I just don't know what we are going to do. Mother said we will end up in the poorhouse," she cried.

Daniel had an idea, but before he told her of his plan, he went to look at the empty shop and flat the following day. It needed cleaning and fresh distemper on the walls. Daniel and Adele enjoyed the challenge, their love deepened as she was grateful. The flat looked nice once their furniture had been brought in. Mrs Willows grudgingly thanked him, though she obviously felt they had been dropped to a low point living here.

When Mrs Willows was well, she had helped in the shop while

Adele was busy making ladies' dresses for women who could afford it. Daniel managed to find her bales of silk now and then on his travels; lace and cotton also found its way onto the cart.

He was brought back to the present when Mrs Willows called for assistance. Adele rose, going to the stairs. Daniel said he would take the horse to the stables. He would need to talk to Hannah. How long had he left her standing there? Maybe she could stay in the cart until he had talked Adele into taking her on.

Opening the door, he was surprised that Hannah was no longer standing in the lobby. The yard gate was ajar. Patting Pinto on the rump, he went into the outer yard with both dogs but there was no sign of her.

"Where the bloody hell has she gone?" he muttered under his breath.

Going back to the horse, he removed him from the shaft. The yard was just wide enough to turn him and he led him back the way he had come just an hour or so earlier. Telling himself he had done all he could for Hannah, he felt somehow deflated. Of course he was delighted to be with Adele again but for an unknown reason, he felt a responsibility for Hannah, like he would a sister. It worried him that she wouldn't manage on her own. She would have gone off not thinking of the consequences of her actions as usual.

He would put the word out. Someone would find her. By then Adele might accept the help.

Women! He would never understand them.

CHAPTER EIGHT
SAINT NICHOLAS CHURCH

Walking quickly, Hannah backtracked toward the way they had come into the town, through the square. Turning down another passage, so she would not be seen by Daniel if he tried to follow her, she kept up her pace. Once she thought she had gone far enough, she slowed to look around. Breathing heavily, she pressed on until she came to a river. To the left she saw a church so she continued in that direction. She didn't have a plan but felt at least the church would be a safe place to think. As she walked closer to the church, she saw a huge window on one side although the church wasn't as large as those she had seen on the way to Kingsmead. It looked very peaceful.

Opening the large wooden door, the creaking echoed down the aisle, as did her footsteps. In the rafters she saw angels, arms outstretched playing musical instruments. She chose a pew which was bathed in a golden light from the windows, and sat down. Closing her eyes, she prayed for forgiveness, for help, for her baby and for Daniel. She hoped he would be able to sort things out with Adele.

It was a strange name she thought. Adele Willows, Miss Willows. Hannah didn't know what her married name would be. She had never asked Daniel his surname mainly because she didn't know what surname to use herself as she didn't want any questions about her name. Not her married name of Cloverley as someone might be looking for her. She couldn't use her maiden name of Palmer in case someone knew her father. She settled on her mother's maiden name, Church. Hannah Church. It seemed prophetic as she sat there; it might be a sign.

When she opened her eyes, there were shadows where the sun had once been. She must have been praying for a while. Before she could close her eyes again and clasp her hands together, the door behind her opened. Footsteps sounded down the aisle just like hers had done an hour or so before.

Stopping at the end of the pew, the pastor stopped. "Oh, I am sorry. I didn't realise anyone was here. Do you need any help?"

"No, thank you." She picked up her bundle and walked with him toward the door.

"I haven't seen you here before. Do you have somewhere to go?" He looked her up and down then held the door for her to pass through.

"I'm alright, I just liked the look of the lovely window and wanted to see it from the inside," she lied, turning and walking down the path. Continuing through the churchyard, she knew the pastor was still watching her. She heard the door close so she wandered through the gravestones until she found one without being in view of the path or church. Pulling out the can Mrs Whisker had given her, she gulped the water. She was hungry, her stomach grumbling but she didn't know where to buy food and the sun was dropping quite rapidly. It would be stupid to wander off now, she thought. She would wait for the pastor to leave then try to find somewhere sheltered and dry for the night.

That first night she spent in the doorway of the church wrapping her blanket around her, using the rest of the bundle as a makeshift pillow. The pearl handled gun went back into her dress pocket. She felt safer with it to hand even if she had no shot but anyone attacking her wouldn't know that. The floor was cold as was the wind even though she had wedged herself behind the portico. Anyone looking directly at the door wouldn't see her. She would have to be gone before the pastor came to open the door in the morning.

The cold and her hunger made sleep fitful, bones aching to the point where she wanted to cry out. Her mind was in turmoil; was this what her life was going to be like from now on? She couldn't face it. What did she expect? How would she cope when her baby was born? She would have to find somewhere before the worst of winter came which wouldn't be too long now. Watching shadows creep along the walls, the noises of the night were somehow comforting, owls in the trees, mice scurrying, even barking dogs. At least she wasn't totally alone as the darkness slowly crept into a grey dawn.

Struggling to stand, even when hanging on to the wall, she felt dizzy with hunger. Closing her eyes for a moment until the blood stopped pounding in her ears, she straightened her aching back.

Taking some coins from her purse, she placed them in the pocket of her dress. The purse was placed back with the gun in the middle of the blanket which she knotted as tightly as she could with cold fingers before setting off down the path to the lynch gate and onto the river front.

She stood for a short while to get her bearings. Should she go left or right? Certainly not into the centre of Kingsmead as she assumed Daniel would still be around. She desperately needed to find somewhere she could get something to eat. Looking along the river, she spotted a number of men unloading a boat. They might be able to tell her where she would find a shop. They all stopped their work as they looked at this dishevelled woman.

"Excuse me, could you tell me where I could get something to eat and drink?" Her voice was almost a croak.

"You look perished, lass. Get yourself along there." The man pointed further along the river. "You will be able to get something there. Tell him Simeon sent you then he won't rip you off."

The others laughed in agreement.

Nodding, Hannah walked on, forcing herself to put one foot in front of the other. Coming across a hut with a few wooden tables and chairs, she assumed this must be the place. It had a sort of garden with driftwood placed around but the flowers had been replaced by long dry grass. There was smoke coming out of a chimney. She wished she could go and stand beside the fire to warm herself as her whole body felt as though it was shivering with cold.

"Hello," she called and a small man came out of the door, his face very brown with skin like polished leather.

When he spoke, he showed that he only had two teeth at the front of his mouth. "What can I do for you, girl?"

"Simeon sent me. He said I would be able to buy something to eat and drink. I have money." She held her hand out to show the pennies.

"Well girl, I have plenty of strong tea and herring or maybe oats. What do you say?"

"Tea and oats would be lovely, thank you." She grabbed a chair before she passed out. The thought of herring on an empty stomach made her feel quite bilious.

Wrapping her hands gratefully around the steaming mug, she saw her filthy hands, broken nails, skin around her fingers red raw. She knew she must look a mess. Her hair hadn't been brushed. Her scalp itched as though she was loppy but at least her bonnet hid the worst of it. Her clothes were matted with mud which was cloying around the hem of her dress. Her feet ached, her back ached, her head ached, all she wanted to do was cry or to put her head on the table and just drift off never to wake again. Pull yourself together, Hannah, she said to herself, you've got to get through this otherwise it will have been a waste of time. Your baby needs you to be strong.

The old man brought her a large bowl of oats, a bowl of sugar and a spoon. She wanted to grab it from him, to shovel it into her mouth but she stopped herself. Just a few mouthfuls at a time, savour it, she thought, don't let your stomach reject it. All the words were going around her head. Leaving her to her breakfast, the man returned quickly with a mug of tea for himself before taking a seat opposite her.

"What you doing round here, girl? Ain't never seen you before."

Hannah put a spoonful of breakfast into her mouth. "I'm looking for work and somewhere to stay," she said around the mouthful of oats. "Do you know anyone who might take me on?"

"There's nowt round here, girl, mostly fishing and the like, are you any good at that?"

"No, I've never been in a boat. I think I would be frightened. I can't swim." Scraping the bowl, she wanted to lick it but licked the spoon instead.

Pouring her another mug of tea before lighting his pipe, the old man settled more comfortably in the chair. She knew he was going to start asking questions but as she had nowhere to go, she also sat back waiting for him to speak. A little while later, the three men from the boat joined them and she was given a further cup of tea.

"What kind of work you looking for, girl?" one of the fishermen asked.

"Well, I'll try anything. I can clean and cook. I've worked in an inn." She knew she was stretching the truth a bit there but what else could she say?

"Looks like you need a husband rather than a job," one of them said.

The men laughed.

Struggling to understand the men's strong accent, she just smiled at them. She continued to sit as the sun rose in the still grey sky. In the shade, the temperature was quite cool so she pulled her shawl tighter around her shoulders. How many times over the last few weeks had she wished she had worn her coat the day she went to market with her husband? It was only a light coat but it would have given her some warmth. She would need to find a clothes stall soon but her priority was to find somewhere to live and work. Her money wouldn't last too long if she couldn't do that.

Eventually the fishermen stood to leave. "Good luck, lass," one of them said as they went back to their boat.

Putting her penny on the table, she thanked the old man before heading in the direction of the fishing village. The oats had temporarily halted the gnawing hunger in her belly though she knew it wouldn't last long. Her baby was kicking, demanding more. She needed to eat to help it to grow. She didn't know much about pregnancy, she had lost her first two babies early on and she certainly didn't want to lose this one now. It was all she had of her own.

Hitching her bundle onto her hip, she walked toward the first row of huts which looked like dwellings. She realised the houses were in a row, back to back, a lane with shops on the opposite side backing onto the river.

Here goes, she said quietly to herself, start at the first shop and ask about work while pricing up the food.

The first one was larger than it looked. It went back a long way, ending at a counter where a woman looked up as she entered.

"I'm wondering if you have any work," she said, "or if you know anyone who is looking for someone. I will try anything."

"You're not from round here, are you, girl? There's no work for the likes of you round here. We look after our own." With that, the woman turned away.

Hannah tried a few more shops with the same result and was on the verge of giving up when she spotted a bakery. Looking in the small window, her stomach growled. It was as good as anywhere to buy some bits and pieces for later.

"Mister, I'm looking for work, if you have any." Her voice sounded as desperate as she felt.

"Sorry, can't help you, can't pay anyone for work," he said almost apologetically.

"I'll do it for bed and board if you can find something, anything, Mister. I'm a good worker."

"Sorry, I've nothing for you. Try the town, lass, you might have better luck there."

It was getting late. She would need to get some food for later so she held out a tuppence piece. "What can I buy for this then, Mister?"

He must have felt sorry for her because he filled a paper bag with more than the tuppence worth, a current bun, bread rolls and a pie with a broken lid. She nodded a grateful thanks and left.

Deciding to head off back towards the church, she walked as quickly as she could to keep warm while nibbling on one of the bread rolls.

Although she didn't relish the church doorway again, she hadn't found anywhere else that was dry and safe. It must be late afternoon, she thought, as the sky was darkening. The sun had dropped below the buildings of Kingsmead and the temperature dropped with it.

Not knowing if the pastor had left for the day, she tried the door. It was locked. It was going to be a long night if she tried to settle down now but she didn't know what else she could do. In the end, she wandered around the gravestones reading the names until it was too dark to see.

CHAPTER NINE
THE WORKHOUSE

Settling herself in the same corner as the night before, she waited for sleep. The wind was now howling through the trees, trying to rouse souls from their slumber. The groaning got louder as the night sky darkened. Sleet tapped on the wooden doors, like long nails on icy fingers, rap, rap, rapping. She couldn't stand it, wanted to scream out. Her teeth chattered as she shivered from head to foot not only from the cold but from the unknown. Her mind was in turmoil again, fearful of what was to come. She was sure she could hear moaning or whispering coming from the graveyard.

Wrapping the blanket tighter, knees bent so her legs were tucked under her dress and underskirt, just like that first night when she had slept in the woods, she tried to slow her breathing. Closing her eyes, she whispered to herself that she would be alright if she could just get through this night.

The storm carried on unabated. She was cold to her being. It seemed to run up and down her spine. Those long icy fingers grabbed at her neck where her skin was open to the elements between her bonnet and her shawl. She wanted to shout for help but there was no living soul to hear her, only the dead and she was afeared. She had known this feeling before, this squeezing of her throat until she lapsed into a dead faint.

This was how the pastor found her the following morning as he hurried to open the church doors, his collar pulled up around his ears. His coat was soaked even though his walk was a short one. The blanket still wrapped around her was wet. He was afraid she was dead, looking at the grey pallor of her face, her hands icy as he placed them in his. He called to the gravedigger to come and help him to carry her to the workhouse infirmary.

The nurses looked at this pitiful girl who was delirious, moaning, her temperature sky high. Taking her wet clothes from her, they washed her in tepid water to slow the fever while cooling the skin.

How long had passed, Hannah didn't know. People came to check on her, bathe her, feed her weak soup but they all seemed to wear the same vague face. It was their hands and voices which were different. Some gentle and soft, others brusque and sharp.

Hannah didn't care. This white blank space she was in was warm and comfortable and there was no one in this place but her. Her days dissolved into night and back again. Her eyes remained closed. It was too much effort to open them.

Someone had taken her hand and was praying quietly. She wasn't ready to open her eyes but it was soothing to hear his voice. She wanted to stay cocooned in this place a little longer, wherever it was. Her mind wandered. Had she died and gone to heaven? Had she been forgiven by God for what she had done? Her unborn baby would be with her always. She wanted to see what this paradise was like. Her eyelids fluttered open but closed again at the brightness.

"You're awake, that's good," the voice said. "Don't try to move. You gave us quite a scare." The voice was pleasant.

Turning her head, Hannah opened her eyes again. The pastor smiled. She tried to speak but no sound came. Licking her lips, they were dry and cracked. There was a taste of blood as she swallowed. "What's happened to me?"

"You almost died in the storm. You have been away from us for quite a while. Let me go and let someone know you are awake." He stood, letting her hand fall onto the dark grey, coarse rough blanket.

Opening her eyes fully, she tried to look around. Her hearing had come back, no longer a silence. She could hear people in the other beds. She heard a door opening and shutting in the distance.

Stretching her legs toward the bottom of the bed, she placed her hands on her stomach. Though her baby was quiet, she could feel it moving.

A nurse bustled to her bed, talking animatedly to the pastor. "Let's sit you up," she said, plumping up the pillow. "You might feel a little dizzy but it will soon wear off." Turning her attention to the pastor, the nurse said, "I'll see if I can find something to eat for our patient. Can I bring you a cup of tea?"

"Yes, very kind, thank you."

When she and the pastor were alone, Hannah spoke. "What's happened to me? How long have I been here?"

"Let's get the introductions out of the way first. My name is John. I'm the pastor from St Nicholas Church. Do you remember we met there?"

"Yes I do. I'm Hannah." She paused. Was it a sin to lie to the clergy? "I'm Hannah Church."

Shaking her hand, he continued. "You've been here for six days, it's November 8th."

"Oh well." She tried to smile. "I've missed my birthday. I was twenty one on November 6th."

"Well, belated happy birthday to you. Is there anyone we can contact to let them know you are here?"

"No, no one, I have no family." Again she lied. "I came to Kingsmead to look for work but I need to find somewhere to live."

"Ah, here's your lunch, Hannah. Can you manage?"

She picked up the spoon trying to eat some of the very weak broth in front of her. She only managed a few spoonfuls before feeling exhausted. Closing her eyes, she slept again.

The nurse and the pastor walked over to the desk which was at the centre of the ward which held sixteen beds. It was full of people needing care, some close to death, others wishing they were dead.

The nurse spoke first. "Who do you think she is and where has she come from?"

"Said her name is Hannah Church. Her accent isn't local. Said she has no family and is looking for work in the area."

"Her belongings include a gun, a wedding ring and also a purse with money which we recorded as twenty-five shillings and fourpence. Quite a lot for sleeping rough, don't you think? Once she is well, she will have to leave. She can't go into the workhouse, and she is not destitute nor is she of this parish," the nurse said.

"No, you are correct, of course. Can you keep her for a few more days and I will see if I can find somewhere for her? Perhaps I can encourage her to make a donation for her care. Would that be acceptable, nurse?" He stood, wanting to take his leave.

"I'll do my best as always but it will have to only be for a few days, mind. Though where she can go when she is pregnant I don't know."

"I'll pray for her," the pastor said as he left the room. He didn't like Nurse Mary. He thought she was too sanctimonious and pious which was a strange feeling coming from him, a man of the cloth.

Over the next few days, Hannah got stronger. Someone had helped her bathe and wash her hair, and with scrubbed hands and feet she felt much better. Her belly was now swelling with the food, meagre though it was, and her baby was kicking.

Several times a day she walked the corridors, sometimes with Pastor John who she found pleasant company. Her eyes grew wide in disbelief when he told her about the Turkish bath which had just been introduced by the Chief Medical Officer who believed it would provide many health benefits for patients. Most of the nurses, he said, were not trained but were originally from the workhouse itself having found themselves widowed or destitute.

She also found him very knowledgeable about the Poor Law, explaining that as she didn't belong to the parish, she wasn't entitled to relief though he could make arrangements for her to be returned to her home parish for help if she wished.

Keeping to the same lies as before, she said she was a widow, her husband had died and his parents had thrown her out. Her parents were dead and she had no other family. Knowing he would have knowledge of her belongings, she explained she had taken the gun as protection while on the road. This was why she had hidden her wedding ring, in case of robbery. The money was from working at the Green Man in Dealham, he could check with James and Primmy if he wished. She omitted to tell him about Daniel or the fact that she had sold her husband's horse. Keep it as simple as possible, she thought, she would need a good memory if she expanded her lie. She also said, smiling, that she wouldn't get relief in her own parish because, as he said, she wasn't destitute.

Instead he asked her if it was possible to return to the Green Man now she was better. Hannah told him they had asked her to leave when they realised she was pregnant so no, she couldn't go back. With that, she turned and walked back to the infirmary. She didn't want to answer any more questions and he knew that.

It was the 12th of November. Snow had threatened all morning though the flurries were held off by the bitter wind. She had been given a coat which wouldn't fasten over her bump but it kept her back and shoulders warm. She couldn't bear to think where it had come from, someone might have died in it. She shuddered at the thought. It had odd buttons which she had sewn on herself as well as mending the numerous holes in her stockings. She was ready and waiting for Pastor John to collect her but he was late. Hannah sat on a chair by the entrance to the workhouse with her belongings. Someone had already taken her bed. Still feeling quite weak and tired, she was frightened about what would happen next. She knew it would be an effort to fit into wherever she ended up but her time in the infirmary taught her that there were people far worse off than her.

CHAPTER TEN
THE PASTOR AND NORTHEND VILLAGE

John, as she thought of him, carried her bundle as they walked past the church. In its shadow were the houses and shops in which she had asked for work just a few weeks ago. Keeping up the conversation as they walked, he explained that the church was dedicated to the fishermen. Although it was a district of Kingsmead, he said the people rarely ventured out of the area apart from taking fish to sell at the weekly market. Hannah nodded but said nothing.

He called out when they reached the door of one of the wooden houses. "Annie, Annie, we're here," he called, whilst pushing the door open.

Hannah was surprised by the number of people. It was standing room only with women and children. Once the introductions were over, he made to leave, saying, "It's bed and board, Hannah, but you'll be well looked after. I'll see you at church on Sunday, will I?"

"Yes, of course and thank you. I am very grateful, thank you."

"You'll not be thanking me when you see what Annie's got lined up for you." He nudged Annie before going out into the dark.

Her room was little more than a cupboard which had previously been used to store items judging by the number of nails on the wall. Her bed was a wooden pallet with a tick-covered straw mattress. All she could think of was at least it was dry. There was a very small window at the top of the wall though it wouldn't open. The only other source of light was around the door frame which led from an equally small room containing numerous shelves, holding pots and pans above a sink with a cold water tap. Hannah had to walk through it to get into her tiny space. The main room had a stove which at least made the room warm. The stench of fish was almost unbearable for her. It permeated everything, clothes, hair and skin, but she knew she would have to get used to it.

Over the next few weeks, she struggled to understand the conversation as the women's accent was difficult and they all talked very quickly, almost as one. They all looked very similar which she later found was due to the family's closeness. Most of them were first cousins who married but they were all cared for by one another. If any of the men were lost at sea, orphans would be taken into the family while widows were supported. This made it difficult for her to remember who belonged to who as well as who lived where, as they seemed to wander into each other's houses all day. This was why they said there was no work for her, they all worked for each other.

They had their own style of dress very different to what she was used to. The men wore jumpers known as 'ganseys' which the women knitted, the pattern apparently depicting which village they came from. They wore moleskin trousers which they wore even when they were not at sea. The women wore long black skirts, shawls, and the same style cap as the men and were often seen sitting smoking clay pipes while mending nets. The women's hands were never still. In the evenings, they would sit knitting the 'ganseys' in a deep shade of blue. The bigger children went to the village school while the younger ones were often looked after in a sort of nursery by one or two of the women.

They soon helped her to fit into their daily routine by teaching her how to repair the nets with a wooden needle though it was shaped differently to the needles she was used to. They laughed with her when she made a mistake. They had given her a work skirt to wear but it had to be taken out to cover her growing belly as her waist seemed to have disappeared as she got bigger. Some of them would put their hands on her stomach saying "not long now".

She didn't want to admit that she was petrified of giving birth.

Sundays were her favourite day. She looked forward to attending church, seeing John, though he hadn't been to see her. Maybe he was busy or just letting her settle in, she thought. Helping at the Sunday school, she had made a friend of a young girl named Margaret known as Maggie, who told her excitedly that she was to marry in two years' time, to Simeon's son, Arthur.

After the church service on Christmas Eve, there was a small market. They were selling a multitude of things, including a stall with toffee apples and one with roast chestnuts. Hannah bought a toffee apple for each of Annie's grandchildren and a bag of chestnuts to share with Annie when they got home. It seemed the whole village attended church on Christmas Day, even the men. John had given her a pair of warm gloves, and she apologised for not thinking to buy him anything.

"Maybe next year, Hannah," he said, taking her hands in his.

Blushing, she turned to head for home with the others, Maggie linking arms with her, laughing.

People spent the day with their immediate families which seemed difficult to arrange. New Year, on the other hand, was a village affair. All the doors were open as people wandered in and out, having a drink and a bite to eat. Some of the young men in particular seemed to be more inebriated than others which she didn't like. Just before midnight, the men stood together in the middle of the square, a piece of coal in one hand, a small piece of fish in the other. At midnight, all the boats on the river sounded their horns as the church bells rang out to welcome in 1864. The men went to each house in turn wishing the family a happy and prosperous New Year.

Hannah loved it. For the first time since she had left her mother's side, she felt as though she belonged, that she was welcome. The only fly in the ointment was she had overheard that John was giving Annie a few pennies now and then to pay for her keep. She would have to speak to both of them soon but she wasn't sure what to say. However, she didn't get the opportunity to speak to either of them.

Three weeks into the New Year, she awoke with terrible backache.

Annie laughed and said, "It's your time, lass."

"It's too early," she panicked.

"Well, it's God's decision when he wants them to arrive, nothing we can do about it."

Her back ached all day, at times worse than others. She tried putting her hands on her back to relieve it. She wasn't comfortable sitting or standing.

"How long will this go on, Annie?" She was almost in tears.

Annie took her hand. "Lass, lass, did your ma never talk to you about childbirth? It could be days but you haven't started proper yet."

Groaning, she went to sit down, jumping when Annie shouted, "Walk about, Hannah. Look, go to Maggie's and tell her ma you're nearly on your time. She'll come and sit with us tonight."

After putting on her coat, Hannah had only walked a few yards when she felt water trickling down her legs. She couldn't control it even when she tried to hold her stomach in. It wouldn't stop but just kept coming.

"Annie, Annie," she screamed as she doubled up in pain.

Her bed was being moved into the bigger room. Annie shooed the boys out saying, "Go and get Nancy, quick now."

They both looked at her as she held on to the door frame.

Annie helped her to get out of her clothes and into an old nightshirt before placing some old sacks onto the mattress. Water was put on to boil. It wasn't long before she started screaming, only stopping to breathe before screaming again. She screamed for her mother, God and her mother again. She had grabbed Annie's hand so tightly that she joined in the yelling. It seemed like hours. It was hours. The pain was unbearable.

She was covered in sweat and exhausted. They kept saying push but she had no energy left. The dark night gave way to morning as they told her to give one last push. Her baby was nearly here. Finally on 23 January 1864, her son was born but she hardly had the energy to hold him. He was small, his cry hardly a squeak, struggling to suckle but he was hers and she didn't think she would ever love anyone as much as she loved him.

For the first time in her life, Hannah felt whole. She now knew why her mother had loved her so much. How she would have loved to write to tell her mother about her baby, her grandson. They both slept, her son in her arms.

Her bed was cleaned and put back into the storeroom. One of the men had made a shelf unit out of fish boxes to put the baby's clothes in. His cot was another fish box Maggie and Nancy had covered in material. Hannah had to shuffle round the bed to open and close the door but her son was here, she was happy.

After three weeks of being made to stay in the house, she desperately needed some fresh air. The baby was asleep. Annie offered to look after him for a short while but Hannah wanted him to be with her. Wrapping them both up warmly from the February snow, she walked to the church hoping to see John. She had missed their conversations while she had not been attending church.

As she reached the portico, she looked at the corner where she had tried to shelter. If John hadn't found her, they would both be dead. She knew she would never have managed on her own. She had met two decent men since killing her husband; why hadn't she met one of them sooner, she thought. Opening the door then closing it quickly to keep out the cold, she sat in the same pew as the day she had arrived. Laying the baby on the pew, she got to her knees and prayed. "Thank you God for giving me my precious son, I promise to bring him up on the right path in your name." She begged God to keep him safe and for her to be a good mother.

Sitting back on the pew, eyes still closed, she listened. She badly wanted to hear John's footsteps. She waited until she dare wait no more. It saddened her to have missed John. She more than liked him, she realised, but it could never be. How could she keep a secret like hers from him? Telling him would ruin their friendship and that's all it could ever be.

The following morning, the last of the snow was melting in the sun. The sky was clear and although it wasn't warm, it was pleasant enough. When she told Annie she was taking the baby out again, she was told she was out of her mind when he was so small. Yesterday was bad enough but at least she had only gone to the church. But Hannah wanted him with her. She couldn't explain why but she didn't want to leave him.

Walking through the streets of Kingsmead, she thought how much had changed, how grown up she felt now she was a mother. This was the first time she had been to the centre of town since leaving Daniel. The buildings still fascinated her. One day she would bring her son and they could look round together.

The Town Hall was a tall imposing chequered building with a steep arched roof. The steps to the doorway were wide, giving the impression of grandeur.

As she entered, the clerk sitting behind a large wooden desk looked up at her but didn't speak.

"I want to register my son's birth," she said, looking directly at him.

He made her feel like a piece of dirt on his shoe as he pointed down the corridor, wrinkling his nose as he did so. He then returned to look at the paperwork on his desk.

The registrar looked somewhat kinder as he held a chair for her to sit on the opposite side of the desk to him. He explained that he would ask her a number of questions to write in the register before he wrote out the certificate. Any words he wasn't sure of, he would ask her to spell.

"When and where born?"

"23rd January 1864. Northend, Kingsmead."

"Name?"

"Daniel."

"Sex?"

"Boy."

"Name of father?"

She didn't know what to say, she couldn't use her husband's name. The clerk coughed. "Do you have a marriage certificate, Madam?"

"I do have one. My husband died. I don't have it here in Kingsmead." She explained that she had left his family and had no paperwork, nor would she be able to get hold of it.

"I'm sorry, Madam, but without your marriage certificate or your husband's death certificate, I cannot enter a father's name on the birth certificate. Were you married in this parish?"

"No, I wasn't, but I was married, I really was. My husband died and I was thrown out of his house."

Coughing again, the clerk said it would have to be omitted from the form. He continued.

"Mother's name?"

"Hannah Church."

"Address of informant."

"Plot 6, Northend, Kingsmead."

After signing the book to certify that the information was correct, she tried not to cry while she waited for the clerk to return with the birth certificate.

"Madam, if you manage to get hold of your marriage certificate or a letter from the clergy who married you I can, at a cost, amend the certificate for you."

After handing over the money, the clerk passed her the certificate and opened the door for her.

She was distraught. She had registered her son without a father. His father was dead, she had killed him and now her son was a bastard. It made her look like a whore. What was worse she had registered him with the surname Church, now he was Daniel Church. God would punish her, she was sure. She hadn't thought of the consequences of this. What had she done? Her poor son. Her baby was a bastard.

CHAPTER ELEVEN
THE MEETING

Hurrying back through the town, she heard someone shout her name but she didn't slow down. She didn't want to speak to anyone. She was too distressed but they persisted in getting closer.

"Hannah, it's Daniel. Wait."

Stopping, she turned, tears falling, hugging her son closer.

He looked as if he was about to say, "How are you?" but instead said, "What's the matter? I don't want to upset you but I have been worried about you. Is this your baby?"

Nodding, she cried even more.

"Look, come on, you never did meet Adele. I'm sure she can rustle up a cup of tea."

He took her, steering her in the direction of the shop. She didn't resist but walked along meekly. They didn't speak again until they had removed their outdoor clothes. Calling upstairs to Adele to tell her they had a visitor, Daniel pulled out a chair opposite her and sat down.

"Before you tell me what's wrong, tell me who this is?" he smiled at her.

"This is Daniel and he is three weeks old."

"Why did you call him Daniel?" he asked.

"You were the first man I had met who was kind to me, unlike my father or husband. I hope my son will be many things but especially kind." She started sobbing again at the thought of the birth certificate.

Adele barged into the room, obviously having heard what Hannah had said. "Well, well, so this is the young lady, my fiancé is always talking about, is it? I was beginning to think you were a figment of his imagination."

It was the way Adele spoke. Hannah disliked her immediately, wanting to ask when they had become engaged but Adele's look told her to be quiet.

The silence was deafening so she held out her hand which wasn't taken. "I'm pleased to meet you. I was very fortunate when I met Daniel. I think we would have died without his help."

"Adele, do you think you could make some tea? Hannah looks frozen." Daniel smiled at her.

"Don't go to any trouble on my account. I'll have to be getting back soon," she interrupted.

"Don't worry, I won't." Adele marched out.

"So, why the tears?" Daniel said as her son opened his eyes. He took him from Hannah just as Adele returned with a tray.

"This is cosy, just the three of you. I feel like an outsider in my own home," she said, banging the tray on the table. "I'm sure mother would be glad of my company." She barged out again.

"I'd better be off," Hannah said, feeling uncomfortable. "They will be getting worried."

"No, Hannah, she forgets this is my house. You are my guest. Now pour the tea and help yourself to cake while you tell me why you are upset." Daniel watched as the baby wrapped his hand around his finger.

"I've been to register his birth but couldn't use my married name, well, you know why and anyway I don't have a marriage or death certificate. I've used the name Hannah Church. It was my mother's maiden name. I didn't think of the consequences. People will think I'm a whore and now he's a bastard." She started crying again, wiping her nose on her dress sleeve. "It's not right and it's not fair on him. This is all my fault."

"We both know that's not true and you can explain what happened when he is older. Now come on, you know I'm no good when women cry. When you've finished your tea, I'll walk you through town. No arguments, partner."

They both smiled.

Daniel carried the baby as they walked through the streets. It didn't seem to bother him when people stared or when one or two acknowledged him.

Hannah looked at him. "I hope you and Adele won't argue. That wasn't my intention."

"Well, it will give her something to feel superior about. I won't let it worry me. I'll be off on my travels again soon now the weather's better so she will have time to think about it."

Handing her the baby, he took a shilling out of his pocket. "Here, silver for luck, take it for his future. Look Hannah, if you ever need help, write to Mrs Whisker or James, they'll let me know."

"Will you tell them about my son and thank them again for their kindness, Daniel?" she pleaded.

Daniel lent toward her to take a look at the baby. "I will. He's a little smasher, Hannah. Take care of yourselves."

Hearing quick footsteps, she thought Daniel was coming back. She stopped to wait for him. She was surprised when she saw John striding toward her.

"Hello, Hannah. How are you? By, he's a bonny boy." He slowed his stride to hers.

"I'm fine, pastor. We both are."

"Have you been looking round the shops in the market?"

"I've been to register Daniel's birth and we both needed some fresh air."

"Will I see you both on Sunday, Hannah?"

"Yes, of course. I need to speak to you about Daniel's baptism, pastor. When would be convenient for you?"

"What about after Sunday school? I have a few minutes to spare then." He sounded somewhat abrupt.

"Yes, if that's convenient for you," she responded, leaving him standing there as she set off back to Annie's.

All three households were unsettled by the events of the day.

Daniel had seen a man hiding in a shop doorway. He had spotted him coming from the direction of the workhouse and noticed because the man had stopped dead, almost in mid-stride while looking directly at them. Daniel was about to comment on it when the man disappeared, only to be spotted again when they neared Northend. Leaving Hannah at the edge of town, the man caught Daniel's eye again as he slipped into the door of a tobacconist, making a poor attempt to hide. Daniel didn't look toward him as he walked past the shop but carried on at a quick walking pace through the alley which would take him back to the square.

Doubling back, he watched the man catch up with Hannah. She seemed happy to see him so Daniel went into the tobacconist to see if the owner knew who the man was. It settled his mind to find it was actually the pastor from St Nicholas Church.

His problems with Adele were not so easy to fix. She shouted and cried then shouted some more and he let her. In a way he felt sorry for her. If he walked away, who would take her on with her mother and no dowry. She would probably end up an old maid. He wasn't blowing his own trumpet there. She had no friends, she never saw anyone. People had stopped coming into the shop, no one called on her mother. She was stuck there day after day with that old witch.

It was the reason he kept putting off setting a date for the wedding. He was sure he loved Adele but wasn't ready to give up the life he had, the freedom, catching up with friends from around the county. Sometimes he thought he should rebuild Albarn Tamblyn's cottage in the woods on the fens and live a solitary life like Albarn had.

Staying a few more days in Kingsmead, he made his peace with Adele, wishing her mother good health before he was on his way. The latter he prayed for. Once the old bat was gone, there would be nothing except propriety to stop Adele naming the day. He was happy to be friends with Adele again but his mind was on Hannah. She looked lovely as a mother; there was a glow about her. She didn't seem to have a bad bone in her body unlike Adele, he sighed.

In Pastor John's house, it was a different story. He was puzzled about Hannah. She said she had no one but seemed very close to this dark-haired man. She was also happy to let him carry her son which was odd in itself. He didn't know many men, or any men, who would walk around town carrying a child that wasn't their own. When he had discreetly asked around town, no one knew, or would say, who this mystery man was.

Hannah was just as evasive and never mentioned the man at all. When she came to talk about Daniel's baptism, they almost came to blows. There was a determination in her he had never seen before. Once he had looked at the birth certificate, he sighed. "Hannah, I'm sorry, truly I am, but I can't baptise your baby in the church if there is no father's name on the birth certificate."

"But you know why, pastor. I explained that without my marriage certificate or a letter from the registrar who married us I wasn't able to put his name on. What could I do?" She was biting her lip to stop herself from crying.

"Well, I could write to the parish vicar who married you on your behalf asking him to provide details if you would like me to."

"No, it's impossible. I don't want my in-laws to know where I am and they would find out. They would try to take my son and I can't take that chance."

"It's your choice, Hannah, but I can't baptise your baby. The church won't allow it."

"God isn't very just then, is he, pastor? To take it out on an innocent baby. I'll find a church who will welcome us." Picking up her gloves, she left him open mouthed staring at her.

He sat with his head in his hands. What on earth was going on? He had feelings for her, he knew that. Yes, he was older but there was a spark between them as well as a fight in her that he admired. To marry a widow with a young child would have been acceptable, admired even by the church, he was sure. Now it could never happen. He realised he didn't know anything about her and what was worse, their friendship would never recover.

Hannah had returned to Annie's fit to blow, brushing the questions off. There was to be no christening at St Nicholas Church now or ever, end of story. She would say no more, as she bustled around in a temper.

"Give over lass, you'll break something," Annie said. "Now either tell me what's got you into this state or get over it."

"Sorry, Annie, I'm fine. I will get over it, I promise you."

Get over it she did with a gusto her mother would have been proud of. She saw John each Sunday continuing with the Sunday school but, apart from a cursory handshake for appearances, they didn't speak. She was perturbed when her things seemed to have been rifled through in her room. She couldn't prove it, so she said nothing. She made sure her things were better hidden, assuming the birth certificate had been looked at.

Baby Daniel thrived. No longer the weak sickly baby, he had chubby legs which he was trying to stand on. His cheeky smile lightened her heart. She was pleased he looked nothing like his father; she hoped he hadn't inherited his cruel streak.

Her daily walks with him put colour in both their cheeks. It took her around the village and she was amazed at how diverse it was. As well as the general store and bakery which she knew about, there were boat builders, sail makers, chandlers, rope and twine makers all along the riverfront. Each skill had been passed down through the generations. She loved chatting to the men as they worked. The village also had a public house which was used for all the gatherings, weddings and funeral wakes of the whole village. The school was well attended, and a new classroom was in the process of being built to accommodate the increase in the number of children in the village.

The school board had interviewed several people for the role of primary school teacher, all men from outside the district, but Hannah was also observed in the classroom where she helped out.

The first man to be offered the post turned it down when his wife visited the village. The second man only stayed for a few months after running up a huge bill in the bar. Hannah was asked to step in on a temporary basis which was ideal for her. It was a salaried post which was paid at the end of each term. Nancy had agreed to look after baby Daniel for a small fee and she was able to pay Annie for their keep without using any more of her savings.

Absolutely loving the role of teacher, her life with baby Daniel was almost perfect. If she could move out of Annie's storeroom into a place for the two of them and be on better terms with John, she would be very happy indeed.

Occasionally she wished she could write to her mother but she worried about reprisals for them both. It saddened her that her mother would believe she was dead.

Winter ended and spring brought flowers out around the village. Little Daniel grew tall, playing with the other children. Nancy loved him almost as much as her own. Maggie and Arthur married. Hannah was a bridesmaid which she was delighted with. Her dress was a delightful bluebell colour which only enhanced the rich copper colour of her hair and the deepness of her large brown eyes. Everyone was dressed in their Sunday best as the drinking and dancing went on late into the night. Hannah didn't drink nor did she dance. She was asked many times for her hand for a dance but pleaded shyness each time. The thought of a man holding her while smelling of alcohol upset her. Instead she sat with little Daniel sleeping on her knee as she smiled with happiness for her friends. The obvious joy of the newly married couple made her reflect on marriage. Hers had been only pain and fear every day.

The summer was a warm one so she taught the children outside, taking them to the river to see what their fathers, brothers and uncles did. Her life seemed settled.

CHAPTER TWELVE
STAINSBY GAOL

It was the beginning of September 1867 just a few days before the start of the new school term. Hannah had been in the classroom cleaning and setting out the desks and chairs while little Daniel played happily with a slate and chalk. He was covered in the white dust, looking so comical but how she loved him.

Also, Hannah had an admirer on the horizon, Nathan Mays. His wife had died in childbirth not long after Hannah had had Daniel. She liked him well enough but tried to put him off. It could never be without her marriage certificate. The church wouldn't marry them without proof that she was a widow and she certainly wouldn't live with Nathan. That would only add fuel to the fire.

She knew there were rumours about her which she ignored. She couldn't address them and people would think what they wanted to.

Stepping back, she looked at her writing on the blackboard. She had chalked the alphabet ready for the first day. She couldn't do any more today. Putting a coat on her son, she was about to put on her shawl when there was a tap at the door before John entered.

"Hello Hannah." He bent down to see little Daniel, not looking directly at her when he continued. "I've had a visitor looking for you, Hannah."

"A visitor for me? I don't know anyone."

"Well, it seems you do. Miss Adele Willows has been looking for you. Name ring a bell, Hannah?"

"Oh her. Well, I know of her but I wouldn't say I know her. What did she want?"

"Wants you to go and see her as soon as you can. She was in a bit of a state. Do you know what it's about, Hannah?"

She didn't like the way he said her name after each question. It was threatening. "Of course I've no idea what she would want with me. Didn't she say?"

"All she said was to tell you it was to do with a mutual friend. As I say, she wanted you to call as soon as possible. It sounded urgent. You must have some idea what it's about. How would you two have a mutual friend?"

Daniel. She knew it would be Daniel but she tried to look unconcerned and hoped that her eyes hadn't given anything away. "I don't know, pastor. I really don't know but I will call on her tomorrow and sort it out." Then picking little Daniel up, she stood to one side so the pastor could leave the room first.

"There's something odd about this, Hannah, and I'll make it my business to find out."

"Very Christian of you, pastor, I'm sure."

Then she walked out, on her way to Annie's, leaving John open mouthed.

Her initial urge was to walk past Annie's and rush off to find out what was wrong with Daniel but she knew if she did there would be ructions. The pastor was still around and he would no doubt follow her, which she didn't want.

That night, she couldn't sleep, thinking that something terrible must have happened to Daniel, otherwise Adele would never have sought her out. The woman must be desperate to look for her. She would have to go and help Daniel, return the favour. Whatever she needed to do, she would do.

After a very restless night, she was up early. She fed little Daniel before putting on his Sunday best. She didn't want Adele to think her son wasn't looked after.

"Where are the pair of you going this early in the morning?" Annie asked although Hannah guessed she already knew.

"I'm going to see the lady who called yesterday," she responded, hoping this would be enough but knew Annie would have more to say.

"We took you in when we thought you had nothing. Where was this friend then?"

"She's not a friend, I've told you. I only met her once when she wasn't very nice to me so she must be desperate to seek me out. Anyway, the sooner I get there, the sooner I'll be back and then it can be forgotten."

It took her longer to walk than usual. Little Daniel didn't like being carried and struggled to get down from her hip. He was heavy but if he walked, he wanted to stop and inspect everything. Bending down, she put him on her back singing, "Horsey, horsey, don't you stop. Just let your feet go clippety clop," which made him chuckle in delight.

The shop door was locked so she rapped loudly and waited. She wasn't going through to the yard, the tradesman's entrance. Bugger that, she thought, God forgive me for swearing. She was about to bang on the door again when it opened to reveal a dishevelled Adele. It looked as though she had gone to bed with her clothes on. Her lovely blonde hair was uncombed, and there were black shadows under her eyes.

I've got the upper hand here, Hannah thought. She needs me, I don't need her.

"What do you want Adele?" she demanded. "I assume it's something to do with Daniel, else you wouldn't have come looking for me."

Without speaking, Adele opened the door wide to let her pass through. There was no fire in the grate and there were no warming embers to take the chill off the room. It didn't look as though there had been one for a while. The room looked neglected. She supposed Adele spent most of her time upstairs with her mother. In a way Hannah felt sorry for her. Little Daniel struggled in her arms so she put him down, taking his toy rabbit out of her pocket.

"I didn't know who to turn to," Adele said. "Daniel... Daniel is

89

in Stainsby Gaol. I've had word but I don't know anything else. He must have been in there a few weeks. Apparently, he is in a bad way."

"What's this got to do with me?" Hannah said sharply.

"Well, I hoped you would be able to go and find out what's happened. I would go myself but I can't leave mother, you can see how I'm fixed. You said you were indebted to him so I thought you might help. Look, I can give you the money for the train fare and a cab. I am worried, truly I am." Adele took out a handkerchief and wiped her eyes. "Look, I wouldn't ask but I am desperate. Please can you help him? I'm not asking for me. From what I hear, you owe him. Please pay him back for his kindness to you years ago." Adele held out her hand with a number of coins. "There's a train in less than an hour. If you take a cab to the gaol, you will be able to get the four o'clock one back."

Hannah hadn't spoken as she was in shock. She didn't want to go; she couldn't say that she had never been on a train before but she did owe her life to Daniel.

"All right. I'll go and find out what has happened and call in on my way back. I'll have to go and get some milk and things for my son to eat." She bent to pick him up.

"No," Adele said quickly. "You had better leave him with me. I'll take care of him. They won't allow you to take him into the gaol. You'll be quicker on your own." Adele seemed to have it all planned out for her.

"I can't leave him. You don't know how to look after him and he might get upset. I'll take him back down to the river and leave him with people he knows."

Adele picked the little boy up. "He'll be fine. You wouldn't have time to get down to the river and back in time to catch the train. Honestly, I will keep him entertained. I have food he can eat. Please, just go. For Daniel!"

Against her better judgement, Hannah found herself walking toward the train station without her son.

She wasn't happy about it, she wasn't happy at all. Once today was over, she would be even with Daniel and she would feel indebted to him no more.

The train was hissing and belching steam like a huge monster. It frightened her but people were meandering along the platform without any hesitation and that made her feel braver. If they weren't worried then why should she be? She bought a third class ticket and followed the crowd until she found the correct carriage, and climbed aboard. She had only just settled when the conductor slammed the door shut, making her jump. He blew his whistle, waved his flag and they chugged slowly away. She held onto the seat as the train built up speed. The couple opposite smiled at her. Watching the villages and countryside pass by in a whirl, she was fascinated. Perhaps she had been this way with Daniel. They stopped at Dealham station, and she thought of James and Primmy. It would be lovely to bring her son to visit them by train. What a jolly day out that would be for both of them. She would love to see his face when he saw a train for the first time.

It fascinated her that it had taken just a few hours to get to Dealham by train when the same journey had taken days by horse and cart. What fascinated her even more was that, apart from the names of the stations being different, it would seem they hadn't moved at all. The stations were identical with the long platform and a number of stone pillars holding up a roof structure. The stationmaster's office and waiting rooms were in the same place all painted in purple and white. The uniforms of the porters were also identical. The smoke gave the platform an eerie feel like a recurring dream where people travelled but never reached their destination. Even the people on the platform were ghostlike, disappearing into the smoke before reappearing in another place. It didn't seem natural to Hannah somehow.

She was worried about leaving her son with Adele who really didn't seem to be the maternal type but then neither had she before she had little Daniel. She didn't know the woman, which made her feel worse about leaving him. She should have left him with Annie or Nancy but they would have asked too many questions and what could she have said to them? There was no way she could explain why she was going off to a gaol to see a man they had never heard of.

Following the other passengers along the platform towards the exit, she hailed a cab, asking the cost to Stainsby Gaol. While sitting in the cab, she thought this was a day she would never forget in a hurry. It was a day of firsts. She had been on a train, hailed a cab and was now going into a gaol. They were soon outside a large sandstone building where the cabbie doffed his hat as he helped her down.

"Would you like me to wait, Madam? No extra charge."

"Oh yes, thank you."

The walls of the gaol had no windows, only a door which looked tiny in comparison to the height of the walls. The man at the gate took her name and asked who she wanted to see.

"Daniel." She was mortified when she realised that she didn't know his surname. What an idiot. She hadn't thought to ask Adele. She had gone off with only half the information, with no thought of the consequence. What a wasted journey if they wouldn't let her see him.

"He's been in about three weeks. I think he might be hurt. Oh and he has black hair."

Laughing, the guard replied, "Well that narrows it down a bit. Must be a good friend or does he owe you money? Let me go and see what I can find out."

Offering her a seat in a corridor, he set off, his footsteps echoing as he went. She looked about her. The corridor went both left and right before turning so it looked like a blank end. When he finally returned, he said, "I can take you to see the prisoner but you will have to be quick."

"Thank you," was all she could say. Suddenly she was nervous about seeing Daniel again.

Now she could hear both sets of footsteps as they walked along corridors. Now and then she heard men shouting. The walls seemed to be narrowing as they went deeper into the gaol. She could see that this must be an older part judging by the stonework.

Eventually they came to a semi-circle of cells where many men were sitting, standing and groaning. Against one wall was a table with two guards sitting on either side.

"Visitor for Daniel Jerrold," the guard said. "Bring her back to me when she's finished. Good luck, lass."

Giving her a seat at one side of the table, the guard brought out a dirty, dishevelled man covered in blood. One eye was swollen closed. His arm was obviously broken, looking at the way it hung from his shoulder. He shuffled towards her and not just from the shackles around his ankles. She thought they had brought the wrong man until he rasped, "Hannah."

"In God's name, what has happened to you? I hardly recognised you."

"No time to tell you. I need your help."

She moved closer to hear him as he whispered, "I need to pay my fine of fifteen shillings and something to pay the gaolers. Can you get hold of any money? I will pay you back but I have nothing here."

"I'll get it for you. I'll get you out, I promise you. I'll be back to take you home." She took some money out of her purse and handed it to him.

She looked at the two guards and said sharply, "Has this man been seen by a medical officer? Have you never heard of the Prisoner Welfare Act? Now I expect him to be cleaned up and treated by the time I return." She reached for Daniel's hand as they led him away.

What had made her say that? John had talked to her about many things but she did not know whether this Act even existed. She had probably made it up.

"All right, lass?" the gate guard asked as she was about to leave.

"Well, he's in a bit of a state and I need to raise fifteen shillings to get him out. Can you tell me where I can find a pawnbroker?"

"His fine is fifteen shillings but you will also need to pay one shilling and sixpence in court charges on top of that. If you get the money to the court tonight, he will be up before the magistrate tomorrow. The nearest pawnbroker is on London Road. I'll tell the cabbie. He will take you."

The black horse was pawing restlessly at the ground as she climbed into the cab, trying to think what she needed to do. Her first priority was to get the money back to the court. Within a few minutes, the horse pulled up outside a pawnbrokers and the cabbie opened the door before lowering the steps for her.

"Will you wait again?" she asked. "I'll pay for your time."

The man doffed his hat.

This was another first. She had never been into a pawnbrokers before. It certainly was a day to remember. The shop was full of all sorts of interesting things, though it had a smell of cigars, sweat and mould, or a combination of all three. She wondered who would pawn such things as a stuffed fox which was almost threadbare, or a pair of lace gloves, and moreover who would buy them.

The man behind the counter was very short with a pinched face. He was wearing a wig, which had slipped to an unfortunate angle. She stifled a giggle at the thought that someone may have pawned it, as it certainly didn't fit the wearer. She coughed instead.

Taking her purse out of her pocket, she removed her wedding ring. Then she put the pearl handled gun on the counter next to it. This was the only thing she had left of her mother but needs must.

"How much will you give me for these?" She tried not to sound desperate.

The pawnbroker put a magnifying glass to one eye and picked up the narrow banded ring. "Where did you get this?" he said.

"It's mine."

Then he picked up the gun, turning it around in his stubby fingers. "This'll need cleaning. It's a strange thing for a lady," he stressed the word lady, "to carry. Not many women have them now. Do you have a certificate?"

"No, it was my mother's. I've kept it for sentimental reasons but never used it." She wanted to hurry him up as the cab was still waiting.

"Well, I don't know how much you were looking for. The best I can offer without a certificate is twenty-five shillings for the gun and ten shillings for the ring. It's more brass than gold."

She knew she was being done so pretended to think about it, picking up the ring and turning it in her fingers. It was gold, she knew that, so she put it back in her purse. She loathed the man who had given it to her but it wasn't enough to bail Daniel out, even though she would be happy to be rid of it.

"I'll keep the ring," she said finally, "but I'll accept the money for the gun."

The pawnbroker scrawled out a receipt which he handed to her along with a guinea, saying the remainder was for insurance and a retainer. "You've four weeks to buy it back."

"I don't want to buy it back."

"Rules are rules. Take it or leave it. Just put your mark here in the book."

Hurrying out of the shop, she didn't see the pawnbroker watching her from the window as she returned to the cab. What she did notice was an inn opposite the shop. She would need somewhere to stay now she had missed the train.

She paid the cabbie off once she reached the courthouse. It was a short walk back to the inn and she was desperate for some fresh air.

Giving the clerk Daniel's details, she paid the fine in full. The clerk passed her a receipt and said, "He'll be up before the magistrate tomorrow though I don't know what time."

"Can you tell him I'll be waiting for him?"

"You could sit in the public gallery and watch the drama as it happens. A lot of people do."

"Thank you, I'll do that."

She heard a church bell somewhere strike five. She wanted to go home. She was sure her son would be pining for her. Would Adele hug him until he started to close his eyes to sleep? Hannah sighed deeply. She wished she hadn't dismissed the cabbie. She might have made the train but it was no use thinking about that now. She had missed it, and anyway, she didn't know where the station was.

She walked slowly back to London Road. This was the only place she knew and the last thing she wanted was to get lost in a strange town. Having made up her mind, she picked up her pace to book herself a room at the inn before looking for somewhere to have a meal. She couldn't bear the thought of sitting in a bar. It sent a shiver down her spine. Walking past the pawnbrokers, she saw the gun now in the window, the pearl handle gleaming. It was for sale for five guineas.

"That can't be right," she said out loud.

The pawnbroker stared directly at her through the dirty window.

What possessed her, she would never know but she pushed open the door shouting, "You have robbed me. You knew how much that gun was worth. Far more than you gave me!"

Walking from behind the counter, the pawnbroker replied, "I made you an offer, my dear. You accepted. If I get five guineas then it's my lucky day but do you see anyone rushing in to buy?"

Then turning the sign to closed, he opened the door, indicating she should leave. She was an idiot, she wasn't thinking clearly. It was the stress of all that had happened today. Well, all she could do was put it down to experience.

Walking out of the door, she thought, tomorrow Daniel would be free and she could get home.

CHAPTER THIRTEEN
INNOCENT

She was still thinking about her beautiful boy as she stepped into the road to the inn. As she got to the pavement, she heard shouting from behind her. It was the pawnbroker causing a commotion shouting, "Stop thief, polis, stop thief!"

Hearing a policeman's whistle, Hannah turned to see what was happening. The policeman and the pawnbroker were talking animatedly, pointing toward the inn. She looked around but there was no one else in the vicinity.

Striding toward her, the policeman said, "Can I have a word, miss? The gentleman says you have stolen a ring from his shop. Do you have a ring in your possession?"

"Yes, yes I have, constable. It's in my purse. It's my wedding ring."

"Let's go over to the shop. I am sure we can sort this matter out without the audience." He took her arm none too gently and guided her through the gathering crowd.

The smirking pawnbroker led them back to the counter as the policeman took out his notebook. "I'll ask the lady questions first if you'll just remain silent, sir. You will get your turn to speak."

The questions came thick and fast. Had she been in the shop before? What was the purpose of her visit? While there, did she pick up the aforementioned gold ring?

"Look, constable, let me make myself clear. I came into this shop a few hours ago to ask what he would give me for my wedding ring and a gun, which is now in the window. The gentleman," she almost spat the words, "offered me ten shillings for the ring which he said was mainly brass so I declined. He also offered me twenty-five shillings for the gun which he is now selling for five guineas. That's robbery, constable. Here is the receipt for the gun and this is my wedding ring." She placed them on the counter.

The constable turned to the pawnbroker. "Is this true, sir?"

"She's exaggerating the truth. She did come in today and I did purchase the gun from her but she did not offer the ring because it belongs to me, it was here." He pointed to an empty ring box.

"Liar!" she shouted. "You know it's mine. Why would I lie?"

"Would you empty your purse, madam," the constable asked.

Complying, she tipped out the remainder of the money.

"What has happened to the guinea the gentleman says he gave you?"

"I had to pay a debt. I wouldn't have come in here otherwise."

"Look," the pawnbroker said, "that's my ring and I can prove it. It's nine carat gold, with the letters ERC stamped inside. It weighs three quarters of an ounce."

The constable picked it up.

Hannah said, "Of course he knows that. He took it from me to look at before offering me ten shillings, though I am sure it's worth a lot more."

"Can I look at your hands, madam?" The constable was trying to keep control.

"See," the pawnbroker cackled. "There's no mark on her wedding ring finger."

"No, there isn't," Hannah shot back. "My husband died several years ago. He wasn't a nice man so I stopped wearing it." She knew she was getting herself upset. Her answers, although true, sounded implausible.

"Put it on, madam." The constable held it out for her to put on.

She felt humiliated when she couldn't get the ring over her knuckle. She had put weight on since she had last worn it.

"I think you had better accompany me to the station, miss." The constable took her arm firmly again.

Spending the next few hours being questioned about the ring and the gun, she knew she couldn't give them all the answers. Giving too much away would send her to the gallows. She couldn't tell them where she had been married nor the name of her husband. Her silence made her guilty.

Hannah was told she would be up in front of the judge the following day, her cries falling on deaf ears.

They led her to a cell similar to the one she had seen Daniel in earlier in the day.

Two young girls were already in there and a woman was laid on a bed, snoring loudly. She had been charged with being drunk and disorderly, the two girls informed Hannah, saying that they were in there for pickpocketing.

Hannah went over her story again and again in her head and each time it sounded worse than the last. She couldn't tell them her married name or she would be charged not only with murder but also stealing his horse. She could go to the gallows for either. Hannah Cloverley was dead and buried like her husband but it felt like he was still reaching out to her to do her harm. She would have to keep to her name Hannah Church. After all, her son was Daniel Church. The weeping started quietly at first, then came the sobbing. What would happen to her son? She couldn't bear to think about it.

As the evening wore on, the holding cell became busy with busty women. Prostitutes, most likely. Their language was bawdy and they tormented the gaolers who, strangely, seemed to be on very friendly terms with them. During all the loud banter, the drunken lady continued to snore loudly. The two young girls had been locked up many times, they said, their fines would be paid and then they would be out on the street the same day. They might end up with a beating from their uncle but they would soon be pickpocketing again.

The next time a guard came to open the door, with another prisoner, Hannah stood. Rising from a sitting position on the bed, her space was immediately taken.

"Mister, may I have a word with you?" she said.

The women laughed. "Listen to her, all la-di-da, bet she says she's innocent. Well, we all are, darling." They laughed again.

"I know how I can prove my innocence," Hannah said to the guard. "Can I get a message to Pastor John at St Nicholas Church in Kingsmead? He will vouch for me."

"I bet he will," the prostitutes said, nudging each other and laughing again.

"Save it for the judge, lass," the guard responded, walking away.

Crouching in the corner, resting her head on her knees, Hannah closed her eyes and prayed. Please God, I know I keep bothering you but please let this nightmare end soon. Also please, please take care of my baby.

The following morning Hannah was taken with the others to go up against the magistrate in court. She was frantic about her son, and desperately wanted to get home. She would never let him out of her sight again.

By the time her case was heard, it was mid-afternoon. The judge listened to the evidence from the prosecuting witness, the pawnbroker, as well as the constable. Hannah tried to explain to her defence that she had proof of her innocence but he wasn't interested. It had been a long day, he said. His wife had invited people for dinner and he couldn't be late.

The judge deliberated, taking into account all of the evidence before asking if there was anything to add. As no one spoke, Hannah asked if she could speak. She tried to explain that she could prove her innocence. The judge listened to what she had to say but concluded that no one would actually be able to pick out her ring. She may indeed have had one but could she prove without reasonable doubt that it was hers? The prosecution said it was a delaying tactic.

Crying and shouting, Hannah begged him to contact the pastor who could vouch for her good character.

Instead the judge banged his gavel, asking for silence in the court. "I sentence you to be extradited to the penal colony of Australia with a term of seven years before you are eligible for your freedom.

Take the prisoner down to the holding cell. Case dismissed."

Hannah screamed a great blood-curdling scream as she was dragged from the dock, still screaming until she was slapped across the face by one of the women in the cell.

Daniel stepped out of the court a free man expecting to see Hannah waiting for him. His charge as a debtor had been paid in full by her. He would need to find out what had happened to his horse and cart but first he needed to catch the train to Kingsmead. He wanted to see Adele. Hannah would probably have gone straight home, but he wanted to see her. He would need time to get over his injuries. Thinking about her, he tried to whistle through his split lip as he walked to the station.

CHAPTER FOURTEEN
DANIEL'S WEEKEND

Daniel was pleased to be back in Kingsmead although he knew he still had work to do. He had been set up, he was sure of that. He also needed to find Pinto, Laddie and Spot. Someone would have taken them in, he was certain. He had more friends than enemies in the villages. But today, he just wanted to get home, have a good wash and change of clothes. The ones he was wearing smelled awful and they were filthy with dirt and dried blood. He was fortunate he had been in the railway carriage alone.

Reaching the gate leading to the backyard, he heard raised voices and a child crying loudly. Hannah must be here with the boy. His mood lightened though he wondered why they were shouting. On opening the door, the noise stopped. The man in front of him was the pastor who he had seen before. Adele was holding the little boy in her arms, tears rolling down his face. His crying stopped momentarily, though he sobbed, his chest heaving.

"Oh Daniel, look at you!" Adele moved toward him.

"Where's Hannah?" he asked, looking around the room.

The pastor interrupted. "I've been trying to find out but can't get any answers. She said she was with you. If you've harmed…"

"Shut up, shut up! Adele, where's Hannah? What's her son doing here?" Daniel almost spat the questions out.

"She left him with me yesterday when she left to see you. Did you see her?" Adele held the child closer to her.

"Yes, she did see me. She paid my fine yesterday and told me she would meet me after my case but she wasn't there when I got out of court. I assumed she had come back here."

The pastor interrupted again. "I'm in the dark here. What have you both got to do with Hannah? She told me she had no one but then you two turn up and now she's disappeared. Where has she been, and more to the point, where is she? If you've harmed her, I will call the polis."

"Let me sit down while I get the facts." Daniel reached for a chair, grimacing as he sat. He gestured to the pastor to take a seat. "Adele, start at the beginning."

She talked quickly about how the little boy came to be with her and how she had expected Hannah to return on the afternoon train. Pastor John had turned up today, she said, also looking for Hannah. Now he wanted to take the boy back with him but she was refusing. Hannah had left him in her care and this is where he would stay until his mother returned.

Daniel nodded, explaining that he had spoken to Hannah the afternoon before when she visited him in gaol. She must have been to the clerk of the court to pay his fine but that was all he knew. Interjecting, John asked what the fine had been for but Daniel dismissed the question, stating this was irrelevant. They all agreed that as far as they were aware the last person to see Hannah was the clerk of the court yesterday. She would not have stayed away from her son at her own volition.

John stood, stating he would check with the stationmaster on his way home to see if he knew whether Hannah had got off the train. He would let them know the outcome when he sent a boy with a change of clothes for young Daniel as Adele would not consider handing the boy into his care.

If they had no joy, Daniel said he would return to the court on Monday to start looking for her from there although he was sure she would turn up over the weekend. John was emphatic that he would travel with him as Hannah was a member of his parish and it was his duty to ensure she was safe. He was sure something untoward had happened to her and Daniel was responsible. She would never have left her son with strangers and not return.

As he left, he told Daniel in no uncertain terms that he would see him at the station for the first train on Monday morning.

Walking toward the station, John felt he was no further forward with answers as to how Hannah was involved with those two. Especially the man who was called Daniel! Was he her son's father?

If so, why wasn't he on the birth certificate? She had seen the man the day she had registered the birth, he remembered it well. She was in a state then and now she was missing. He was positive that it was all to do with that man. It was a mystery, make no mistake, but he would get to the bottom of it. There was something strange about the whole affair but he wasn't a man to give up easily. He would pray for her.

Daniel tried to give Adele answers but it was proving difficult when his thoughts were on Hannah. He started to shiver with cold but also delayed shock at what he had been through over the last few weeks. His clothes were filthy as was his body which still had the bruises though they were now fading. The gaoler had taken him to see a medic who had cleaned up the worst of his wounds before putting his damaged shoulder into a sling. Some of his ribs had been cracked when he was kicked, he was sure of that, as it hurt when he breathed.

Putting a light to the fire in the small room, he turned to Adele to ask if there was anything in the house to eat. All he wanted was something to eat, get clean and have a warm bed. Going into the yard, he filled up the kettle and a large pot with cold water from the tap but had to carry them separately into the house. Placing them on hooks on either side of the fire which was now starting to blaze, he took the empty coal scuttle to fill it up. However, when he opened the door to the coalhouse, he found very few logs and even less coal and mainly dust. With difficulty, he shovelled what he could into the bucket and returned to the house.

Adele was helping the young lad eat a piece of pie and vegetables which had been warming at the side of the fire. He was sitting on cushions to raise him up to table height, a scarf around his middle that was fastened to the back of the chair to stop him from falling. It was the first time Daniel had seen him in almost three and a half years. The child was no longer a baby but a lovely little boy who looked remarkably like his mother. He had the same large brown eyes with long dark lashes. His copper hair was darker though and curled cherub-like around his face. He didn't seem to be afraid.

Sitting in the chair by the side of the fire, Daniel put his head in his free hand. Adele said his food would take longer to heat through so he just sat waiting for the water to heat up enough to have a bath.

Once they had all eaten, Daniel could have eaten the same again, the meal was so frugal. It wouldn't have been a large meal for Adele and Mrs Willows alone but for four of them, it was a meagre fare. It had never occurred to him how Adele managed for money. He always assumed that they managed on Mrs Willows' pension but looking at the state of the house, they must be struggling. As for Mrs Willows, he couldn't face going up to see the old bat tonight. She could wait until tomorrow for him to pay his respects and wish her good health.

Adele deserved better, he thought. She was in need of a better explanation, which he would give her once he had sorted out a bath and bed.

Standing, he walked slowly into the scullery where he removed the tin bath off the nail on the wall, taking it to the clippie mat at the side of the fire. By the time he had filled a bucket with cold water, young Daniel was undressing while Adele laughed at the boy's antics. Anyone looking through the window at the scene would have considered it a happy family. The little lad seemed to give his love unconditionally and in return people warmed to him. Adele glowed when tickling and drying him while he squealed in delight. He was soon in an old shirt, which had shortened sleeves and the collar removed, ready for bed.

Once the child had been settled in her bed with his toy rabbit, Adele returned to the room with bedding, a clean nightshirt and towel. She lifted the kettle off the hook to top up the bath before helping Daniel off with his boots and socks. She was surprised when he asked her to help him with his jacket and shirt. He told her he would manage his trousers and undergarments himself if she could just help with his top clothes. Trying not to hurt him, she removed the sling from his arm before sliding his jacket down his arms. It was more cumbersome trying to remove the shirt over his head. Wincing and gritting his teeth as he lifted his damaged shoulder, Adele gasped when she saw the strapping and bruising around his chest.

Removing the bandage, Adele said, "What's happened to you, Daniel? Your back is covered in scars. It looks as though you have been whipped."

"That's from when I worked on the wherry," he said. "Adele, do you think you could fill the kettle for a drink while I get into the hot water? If I don't sit shortly, I think I will fall."

When she returned to the room, his eyes were closed. The grey pallor of his face finally had a pink tinge to it from the steam. She rolled up her sleeves before kneeling beside the tub as she picked up the cloth scrap and soap.

"Talk to me, Daniel," she said, taking the cord from his ponytail. Pouring warm water over his hair, she gently massaged his head with soapy hands. The motion of her hands kneading his head and shoulders seemed to release some of the tension in his neck muscles. He relaxed while the knots in his neck and back began to untangle.

He quietly began talking, explaining what had happened to him several weeks before. He had been travelling toward Albarn Tamblyn's old place when he was set upon by a number of men who jumped out of the bushes onto the bridleway as though they had been waiting for him. One of them grabbed Pinto's halter, causing them to come to an abrupt stop. Their faces were covered with a neckerchief and no one spoke.

"I tried to fight them off," he said, "but they hit me on the shoulder with some kind of heavy weapon. I couldn't get to the river. They tripped me and I fell."

Adele made no comment as her hands rubbed the soapy cloth over his chest carefully, watching his face as he spoke.

Continuing Daniel said, "The last thing I remember is the flames as someone set fire to my cart. I must have passed out at that point as I can't remember anything else."

Adele made no comment as her hands gently continued cleaning his fingers, hands and arms on each side, before moving to the end of the tub. She indicated that he should raise his feet to be washed. There were sores around his ankles where he had been restrained. She gasped as he groaned but didn't speak. She wanted him to tell her what was going on without interruption. He didn't wake fully, he said, until he arrived battered and bloodied in Stainsby Gaol. How long he had lain there, he wasn't sure. One of the prisoners offered to pass a message on for him. When he finally stood in front of the magistrate, it was a Customs and Excise man who spoke for the prosecution. He told the court that they had found him on the towpath after being alerted by the smoke from the fire on the cart. Items were scattered about which they believed to be contraband and they removed it.

The rest Adele already knew.

She still hadn't spoken but stood drying her hands on the towel before picking up the kettle of hot water to make a drink, leaving Daniel to continue washing himself. She was shaking while she stirred the tea in the pot. What on earth had possessed her to wash him? Had she no moral sensibility? How naïve was she?

She had been unaware what a man looked like until she saw the little boy yesterday. She didn't know grown men had hair on their chest and she blushed at the thought. They were unchaperoned and that was often the case but certainly not when Daniel was wearing no clothes. So what, no one else had been calling for her hand. If she didn't marry Daniel, she would be a lonely spinster of the parish and she couldn't bear that. Whatever it took to get him to marry her, she would do. She had seen the way he had looked when he realised Hannah wasn't with them even though he had tried to hide it. The look in his eyes said it all and it was up to her to make sure that nothing, not even Hannah, came between them.

Daniel struggled to pull the nightshirt over his still damp skin. He had never seen Adele in this light before. She always seemed so stiff and formal when he placed his arms around her. Managing to climb into the makeshift bed, he smiled weakly as she returned to the room with steaming mugs of tea. She rubbed his hair with a towel but didn't attempt to brush it. She now seemed embarrassed by the closeness.

He spoke in an effort to relieve the unease they both felt at what had happened. "I'll get my hair cut tomorrow, smarten myself up a bit but I think I'll keep the beard. What do you think?" He didn't add that he wanted to ask around to see if anyone knew who had done this to him as well as getting clues about the whereabouts of Hannah.

Kneeling by the bed, Adele placed her head on the pillow beside his. Daniel stroked her hair gently with his good arm.

"We'll be alright, Daniel, won't we?" she asked quietly.

"Of course we will. We'll talk more tomorrow. I'm sorry, Adele, I must sleep."

Neither spoke for several minutes. He closed his eyes and felt Adele move away from him, hearing her skirt rustle as she went out of the room.

Realising he was now alone, his emotions got the better of him. Tears trickled down his face for the life he seemed to have lost. He sobbed loudly into the pillow. As his feelings overwhelmed him, he cried for his father and Albarn Tamblyn as well as Adele. As a child, he had never cried and now the last twenty years overcame him. He couldn't carry on as before without a cart but he also knew he couldn't live in this household. Fresh air was in his blood. He would feel he was suffocating if he stayed here. Tomorrow, he would ask around for work. He was sure someone would have something for him. Before all that, he would find Hannah and bring her home.

Daniel fell asleep thinking of Adele but his dreams were all about Hannah and the terror on her face when she saw him in gaol. It was her sheer determination to help which endeared her to him.

Daniel's weekend was largely uneventful. He had spoken to Adele about borrowing money though he hadn't enjoyed asking. It made him feel beholden to her somehow. She argued that she had little enough money to manage as it was. They needed coal, logs and more importantly, food and where would that money come from, she asked. In the end, he soothed her ego by begging for her help and offering to repay her with interest.

He explained his money was at Albarn's cottage which he needed money to retrieve. She would have to ask her mother, she said, as it was really her money and she was sure she wouldn't be happy about it. Taking her hands in his, he promised that he would care for them all once he was fit and well again. He would need money to look for Hannah, he said, after all she had paid his fine for him. As soon as the words were out of his mouth, he realised he had made a mistake. He almost had to go down on his knees and beg Adele to loan him the money which she eventually agreed.

He managed to escape the confines of the house when a lad brought fresh clothes for young Daniel. Walking through the market place, he gave the boy a penny asking him to let him know if Pastor John had heard anything about Hannah. Although he had a long chat with the men in and around the barber's, no one seemed to know anything about the copper-haired young lady.

Daniel felt better after his haircut. He no longer had his ponytail and his beard had been closely trimmed. His clothes were old but at least they were clean, his boots shabby and worn. They were all he had, the rest having been destroyed in the fire on the cart. Wandering aimlessly around the market square, he wanted to leave it as long as possible before he returned to the house. He managed to arrange delivery of a few bags of coal in return for some work which would appease Adele for a short while.

It had started to rain gently at first then heavier so he had no choice but to turn about and return to the house, feeling it to be just another type of prison.

Young Daniel was playing on the floor with a bowl of water, filling up containers before emptying them out again as he chatted away to himself. Adele was busy making up a pan of vegetable soup when he told her that coal and logs were to be delivered. She smiled at him, all sweetness, thanking him profusely for it. He wasn't sure

what to do with himself so set about clearing out the ashes from
the fire ready to relight it once the logs and coal had been delivered.

CHAPTER FIFTEEN
HANNAH'S WEEKEND

Hannah was awoken early the following morning to a cacophony of noise. At first, she was disorientated and surprised that she had slept all night but the pain at the side of her face reminded her of the heavy slap. She must have passed out because she didn't recognise some of the women who were now talking and moving around.

The gaoler rattled a large number of keys which were attached to his belt by a strong chain, whereupon he unlocked the cell door. Trying to uncurl herself from the foetal position, she found other women had shared the small bed space with her and were also trying to uncurl. Her nose wrinkled at the smell of a bucket in the corner of the cell which was three quarters full. It permeated her nostrils and she knew she would have to use it before too long but there appeared to be no soap or water with which to wash her hands.

A second gaoler brought in a pan and several tin mugs with spoons attached by cord.

"Stand in line," he said gruffly. "No chargin' or spittin' girls. Ye need to get this down yer then yer out of here."

"What's happening?" she asked the girl next to her who only looked about thirteen.

"Looks like we're getting fed before we're moved on," she replied. "You'd best get in line else you'll get nowt."

Standing on numb wobbly legs, Hannah waited her turn for the watery lukewarm gruel. It wasn't very tasty, hitting her stomach like a stone. Once breakfast, such as it was, was over, the women were pushed unceremoniously back into a line while they were told they would need to sign for the return of their personal belongings. She couldn't see what those at the front of the small line collected but the girl in front had a tortoiseshell comb. Hannah looked at the book where all the women had made their mark with a cross.

Looking up, the gaoler said, "Hello there. What are you doing here? Thought you had left with your young man?"

"Hello officer, I didn't recognise you." Pleading she continued, "Please, please can you help me? I've been charged with stealing but it's a lie, I stole nothing. Please mister, I'm begging you, can you help me get out of here? I need to get back to my son."

"I'm sorry, miss, if you have been charged, there is nothing I can do. Here's your purse. Keep it safe. Many of this lot would kill for a penny. Put your mark here." He pointed to her name.

Writing neatly 'Hannah Church', she said, "If they come looking for me, will you tell them what's happened." Tears filled her eyes as she was pushed from behind.

"Aye, miss, I will. Look after yourself."

The line of women moved along the gloomy corridor through an open door where the sunlight made her screw up her eyes. As they adjusted, she saw the black maria. One by one, the eight women climbed up the steps before sitting on wooden benches on either side. Two gaolers got in last as the door swung shut. The only light and air came from a small open window with bars situated on the back door. With a lurch forward, they were on the move.

Some of the women began talking as she turned to the gaoler next to her. "Where are you taking us?"

"We're off to Sheerness in London where you'll pick up your ship," he replied, laughing. "Make the most of it, this journey will be easy compared to the next one."

She didn't want to strike up a conversation with any of the women nor did she want to alienate herself so Hannah closed her eyes to feign sleep. Hands on her lap to keep her purse safe, she listened to the conversation as her head lolled from side to side. She despaired of the situation she was in. She had a little money if she could make her escape and return to collect her son. They could run away, start again where no one knew them. Maybe she could go to James and Primmy's and work for free until little Daniel started school. She stopped herself. What was she thinking? She could never put people who had been kind to her in danger by harbouring a criminal. How would she manage on the run with a child? What a mess. Her life was a mess and it was her own fault.

She had fired the gun that had killed her husband and for the most part she had got away with it. Now God was punishing her for being happy and she had been happy in Northend. Little Daniel had known no other life than with an extended family of sorts who had accepted both of them. Maybe that was it. She didn't deserve to be happy and now God was punishing her. Well, she would take her punishment for what she had done but her baby didn't deserve to be without his mother. She needed to find a way to let someone know what had happened to her but she didn't know how.

She opened her eyes when the horses stopped. They were let out of the cart for vitals. The men were given ale while the women were given water with dry bread and equally dry cheese. It was nice to stretch her legs, her back aching from the jarring on the pitted roads. Looking around, she had no idea where she was. The flat rolling countryside gave her no cover if she tried to run. She couldn't afford to put herself in danger. She had to survive by being cunning. By the time they reached the end of the day's journey, the women were all tired and subdued.

They were led to a small gaol in a small town that someone said was called Commestoft. Hannah had never heard of it and had no idea where she was. The women were shoved unceremoniously into a small cell which held eight filthy straw mattresses on the floor. They were crammed together wall to wall with just enough room at the bottom to walk past. On one side of her was the young girl who was wearing a pair of men's boots which were too big for her. Only one had a lace to fasten it around her ankle. It made her drag the other boot along the ground in an effort to stop walking out of it. Her skirt was dirty and torn in a number of places as was her blouse, the original colour unrecognisable. She wore no coat or shawl nor any kind of covering on her head. The poor girl's face was quite pock marked giving her an odd appearance. She was shaking as she lay on the mattress facing Hannah. Her dirty thumb went into her mouth for comfort.

On the other side was a bawdy woman who had talked incessantly on the first part of the journey. She would be about forty years old but wasn't wearing a wedding ring. This didn't mean much as Hannah realised she could have pawned it. She had seen plenty in the pawnshop. Her clothes were tidy and clean though the seams on her skirt were shiny with years of ironing. Her hands were not manicured but the nails were clipped short and she supposed they must have been clean when she arrived in court. Her hair had been fastened in a bun at the nape of her neck though it was now falling loose at the front. She had no particular feature which would pick her out.

Hannah took off her bonnet placing it at the top of the mattress as her hair tumbled down to her shoulders. She lay quite still on her back looking up at the ceiling trying to formulate a plan but nothing she hadn't already thought of came to her. One of the women might have to aid her if she was to escape but she didn't know who she could trust.

The noises interrupting her thoughts implied that the others had already fallen asleep. As it began to get dark, she wasn't sure if she was asleep and dreaming or awake but she saw a movement by the cell door. Not wanting to lift her head to look closer, she lay still as a man stepped inside, moving deftly by the bottom of the beds toward her. Hardly daring to breathe, he knelt on her mattress as she still pretended to sleep. Putting his hand under her skirt, he moved his fingers along the hem of her underclothes until he reached her knee. Kicking out as hard as she could, she struck him under his ribs as she let out a deafening scream.

It not only woke up the other women but shocked the gaoler before he could put a hand over her mouth. As she continued screaming hysterically, she clawed at the man, drawing blood. Trying to restrain her, he caught the side of her face which left a gouge at the side of her ear and cheek making her scream even more. The other women were now upon the man. In the melee one or two were caught by stray arms and hands. The gaoler, who now had blood pouring from his nose, forced his way back to the door. Blood was oozing from Hannah's face and she tried to stem the flow with the bottom of her petticoat pressed against it. One of the women passed her a grubby rag but she took it gratefully, pressing it against her skin which was smarting.

"Thank you for helping me," she said, nodding to them all.

"We've got to stick together now and be on our guard," one of the women said. "We are family now make no mistake. This won't be the last time we will need to watch each other's backs." The others, including Hannah agreed, as the woman continued, "Let's try and get some sleep, we will need our strength for the days ahead."

Hannah lay in a ball with her hand under her head, listening to the sounds as the women tried to settle again. The shuffling soon stopped as they fell asleep, some snoring more loudly than others.

She thought the woman who had spoken was right. They were all here for different reasons but the eight of them had become sisters, caring for each other. In a strange way, she was glad it had happened as the women were more accepting of her and she no longer felt aloof. One of them had asked if she had really written her name in the book at the gaol. When she confirmed she had, they all asked if she would teach them their letters which she agreed to do. She eventually fell into a light sleep, listening out for any further noises.

It didn't take long for her bones to ache again as they continued their journey the following morning. This time the women chatted to each other about why they had been sent away. The gaoler whose nose had been broken was nowhere to be seen; he probably couldn't face them as they had all laughed. More's the pity, they said, as they wanted to make sure he wasn't capable of attacking other defenceless girls.

Today she didn't need to feign sleep as she joined in the conversation but not the laughter. Her thoughts were constantly on little Daniel. How could she laugh when she was away from her son?

Late afternoon brought them to a dockside, that must have been Sheerness, where they were taken from the cart. She had never seen a river so wide nor ships so large. Even the small boats seemed so much bigger than the fishing vessels in Northend. Men were everywhere, loading and unloading like ants rushing to and fro. Never in her life had she seen so many people in one place.

As she stood with the others on the quayside next to a huge black and brown wooden ship, she wished this nightmare would be over. All she wanted was to wake up with her son by her side in the cupboard at Annie's. She knew though that this was no dream but a reality and this was the ship which would transport her even further away. The ship had three masts. Daniel had talked to her about the wherry he had worked on only having one mast so she knew this ship was much bigger than that.

The women had been shackled together on the quayside but the shackles were removed before entering what could only be described as a large barn, but instead of bales of hay or animals it was partitioned off, with men sitting behind desks at various points. They were pushed toward the first desk where they queued up to state their name and which gaol they had come from. The men measured the women, and weighed them as well as checking their teeth before noting it all on a form. They were given registration numbers which they were told to remember as well as confirming what they had been charged with. Yet again they had to sign a register to confirm the information was correct. Hannah read the details. She was five feet two inches tall, weighed six stone eight ounces, had light brown hair, brown eyes, had good teeth and no tattoos. After reading it thoroughly, she signed her name to the information.

At the next desk, a number of barbers stood behind chairs. Hannah watched as the women in front of her had their heads shaved. Her hair was hacked off in lumps as she cried out in pain when they grabbed chunks, cutting it as close to her scalp as possible. Her lovely hair was in a pile on the floor, she dreaded to think what she would look like now. She wasn't a vain person but her hair had been one of her best features. She had always prided herself on how it shined when she washed and brushed it. Now it was on the floor, curled up like a dead animal. Her heart ached at her predicament.

At the next desk, the women were given a set of clothes each and told to go behind a screen to remove their own clothes. Hannah protested loudly. She was wearing her Sunday best and although it was no longer clean, it was all she had. She had been showing off to Adele just a few days before but no amount of protesting made any difference.

Joining the other women behind a screen, she began to remove her clothing. She took her purse out of her pocket, placing it in between the underclothes she had put on a bench. She had never shown her body to anyone, not since she was a child when her mother washed her. Her figure was boyish almost, her stomach flat with small breasts. No one would have guessed that she had a child and one she was desperate to get back to.

As the women stood by the screen trying not to look at each other, they placed their hands over their private parts as buckets of water were poured over the top. To say the water was lukewarm would have been a lie. It was so cold they all gasped as it was thrown over them. Shivering, they tried to clean themselves before a further bucket of cold water was thrown over them. The small lump of carbolic soap was all they had to clean their bodies and what was left of their hair.

Drying herself unsuccessfully on the hessian towel, her tears began to fall. Hannah knew she really needed to speak to someone. She wasn't a criminal, really she wasn't, but no one would listen. Someone would have to believe she was innocent.

The clothes they had been given were old but clean. Plain cotton underwear was topped with a grey serge pinafore which was scratchy around her neck but it did have a pocket in it at the side where she placed her purse. Once dressed, she ran her fingers through her hair in an effort to stop what was left sticking out at all angles.

Spotting a man in uniform, she started to walk over to speak to him about her situation. He waved her away, sighing. Not his problem, he said. The gaolers who had brought them here were no longer about. Looking around her, there was no way she was going to be able to speak to anyone as they were hustled toward the ship. Her wrists were sore from the shackles. She rubbed her wrists more because she felt nervous and the pain was comforting somehow. The gouge at the side of her face had scabbed over. Although she had washed it gently, she was worried it would become infected.

Some of the women seemed excited, laughing as they walked up the gangplank and onto the deck of the ship. Their laughter stopped when they were shown a hatch where they had to descend down wooden steps into what seemed like the bowels of the earth. There were partitions which made the room smaller where parts held bunks, and others had long tables and benches with a scullery for cooking.

The ship had a strong smell of the sea which was different from the smell of the river in Northend. Here she could almost taste the salt on her lips. In the depths of the boat where they would be living, the smell made her want to gag. Vomit, human excrement, body odour, tar and fear combined in an unbearable stench that no amount of cleaning and fresh air would remove from her nostrils. Any slight breeze was rancid with all those smells. It was far worse than those first few months when she moved in with Annie. She thought the smell of fish which permeated everything in Northend was the worst smell in the world. She was wrong.

On each bunk lay a pillow and a blanket. There were a number of Bibles, Testaments, Prayer Books and Psalters scattered around the beds, though the dim light didn't promote the reading of them. Small shelves by the side of each bed housed a tallow candle which would provide the only light once the portholes and hatch were closed. It didn't take the women long to settle in. After all, they had nothing to unpack. Instead, they all picked a bed and sat chatting for a short while until they heard noise and commotion above deck.

It was the male prisoners returning from work on the docks. They were the ants she had seen bustling around earlier in the day. They had spent their day dredging, unloading or loading the boats. The men had also been kitted out in regulation dress, clogs, jacket, waistcoat and caps though it was difficult to see fully in the gloom of below deck. Their language was bawdy until they realised they had company when it became good humoured, shouting to the women from their room.

During this time, Hannah struggled to remember what day it was. Her concern for her son's wellbeing grew stronger as time wore on. So many questions were going through her mind until she felt her head would burst. As night drew on, she struggled to sleep, wanting to escape this purgatory she felt herself becoming drawn into.

The following morning, each convict was given a tin bowl with a ration of hot gruel including butter and sugar which at least gave it some flavour. They were told that they would all receive a daily ration of bread, butter, beef or pork, as well as vegetables. Occasionally, they would have pea soup and plum pudding. The captain had decreed that the convicts be given a regular supply of lime juice to prevent scurvy. Many of the women felt that they were being well fed and certainly better than in gaol. They were told that they would be responsible for preparing and cooking their own food which they should put together as well as keeping their room and kitchen tidy on a daily basis.

The sailors told them that they would be heading off to Plymouth once everything was set where they would be picking up further convicts and passengers. The hatch was left open for air but Hannah couldn't see what was going on. She could only listen to the footsteps and shouting as the sailors pulled the ropes to hoist the sails. The ship rolled in a gentle motion which was comforting somehow but she knew she had lost the chance to escape for now. Hannah had never been on a boat in Northend let alone a large ship. She felt they would sink even though it seemed to glide along the water. They were allowed on deck so she watched the land on either side of the dock.

As they set off, she watched the men bustling along the dockside. The further they travelled, the landscape became more rural as the river widened until the land on one side disappeared. As the rain started, the women headed back to their bunks where Hannah read to them from the Bible for a little while.

Eventually she put the book down, closing her eyes as she tried to think. She considered asking one of the men for some clothes which she could use when they got to Plymouth and try to leave the dock that way. However, it would be difficult to ask anyone without being overheard and also she didn't know who to trust who wouldn't give her game away. In the end, the opportunity didn't arise as they were confined to their rooms while the boat continued on its journey around the coast. She didn't want to have any conversation with the sailors as they seemed to want to form a sexual relationship with the women, which she didn't want in any circumstance.

By the time the ship was ready to leave Portsmouth on 12 October 1867, there were hundreds of convicts and half as many paying passengers travelling to Australia. It became more difficult to swab the boards, clean and cook with so many people on board but the women with Hannah had already staked a claim to one of the kitchen areas. This caused some problems but was resolved by including the women in the remaining bunks as each room was now full.

The men were chained to their bunks as the ship departed but the women and passengers watched the boat embark on its long journey to the bottom of the world. As the land disappeared on the horizon, Hannah felt like her life was ebbing away. It was as though she was watching the memories of her son drift away like seeds from a dandelion scattered on the wind in all directions, floating teasingly out of reach on the breeze. She couldn't bear it. The pain in her chest was such that she was sure she would die.

CHAPTER SIXTEEN
THE CHASE FOR HANNAH

Daniel called briefly in on Mrs Willows who remained invalided in her bed. The room had an uncomfortable smell of decay and mothballs. It needed a window opening to let in some fresh air but she continually complained of feeling cold though she was swamped in blankets. She wore no rouge or powder so her ghostly white pallor was clearly visible to Daniel. There was a mutual dislike which was clear by the short conversation. Mrs Willows was disturbed by Daniel's attendance while he was happy to make a hasty retreat.

Poor Adele, he thought yet again. How could she put up with that day after day? That woman had taken to her bed with no thought for her daughter's quality of life. She used Adele for even the most basic of functions, doing nothing for herself. No wonder poor Adele seemed short tempered at times. She must have the patience of a saint.

The mood in the household changed slightly over the weekend and he didn't flatter himself to think it was all his doing. The truth was it was young Daniel who had brought life into this mausoleum of a house. The child would barge into Mrs Willow's room unannounced, chattering away to her and she even seemed to enjoy the company of the young boy. At least it stopped her constantly shouting for Adele to attend to her while he was about.

Daniel had spoken to Adele again about borrowing money which she had reluctantly begged her mother to loan him. She had explained why he had nothing and stressed the fact that they had lived for so long rent free in his property until she had finally agreed. However the old woman wanted her pound of flesh, making sure he would pay interest on what she considered was a short term loan. He explained that he would need to go and collect what was left of his belongings as well as making arrangements for the horse and dogs. Someone would have taken them in but they would require recompense from him for their keep. He assured Adele that he had money, hidden at Albarn Tamblyn's cottage, to repay her mother.

He would go and find Hannah, he said, and she could go back with John while he would head off to the fens. He could give no indication how long he would be away as he no longer had his own transport. He would be dependent on friends' generosity or the carriers' cart. Daniel didn't mention that he wanted to breathe in the fresh air, the smell of wet grass and woody fires. In his mind, he laughed at his poetic ramblings which were tinged with sadness at the thought of his life changing forever.

On a dark Monday morning, he kissed Adele passionately before ruffling the boy's hair and then he set off to the railway station. He purchased a single third class ticket to Stainsby. Pastor John was already waiting on the platform where they acknowledged each other with a nod of the head. Daniel had nothing to say to this man though he was sure John had plenty to ask him.

They travelled for over an hour before either spoke and it was John who finally broke the silence. "Do you have a plan?"

"Well, the first place to start would be the clerk of the court," Daniel said. "It's the last place we know she was seen. Then let's go from there." He had the feeling John felt superior to him but if anyone was going to find Hannah it would be him. He owed her.

"Right, yes, that's right," John responded and there the conversation ended.

Walking from the railway station more quickly than his aching bones felt able, Daniel spoke again. "Let me do the talking here. You wait outside."

"Oh no, I'm coming in with you," John said. "I want to know what happened to Hannah. There have been enough secrets and skulduggery already."

Daniel said no more but pushed the door open entering the clerk's office.

The clerk was able to confirm that Hannah had indeed paid his fine but didn't know where she went after that. Both men left the office and walked around the wall of Stainsby Gaol to the small door where Hannah had entered to visit Daniel a few days earlier. They got no joy there either as the gaoler wasn't the one Hannah had previously seen. They decided to walk into the town, both at a loss as to what to do next and headed for the main street.

"Let's split up," Daniel said. "You take one side of the street and I'll take the other. It will be quicker. Make sure you ask everywhere. Meet you…" Looking round, he pointed to the Black Bull, "…there in half an hour."

With that, he strode off, leaving John open mouthed and infuriated.

There was no success for either of them as they walked in and out of the small high street shops. Daniel was about to give up on the search when he reached the pawnbrokers on the corner of the street. The window was actually around the corner and as he looked into the window he saw what he thought could be Hannah's gun. It looked similar but it was difficult to be sure as it was so long since he had seen it and then only briefly. However, there seemed no harm in asking as he had no other leads.

As he opened the door, a bell rang bringing the owner to the counter.

"The gun in the window. Can I have a look?" Daniel said.

"Ah, good choice, sir. Is it for a special lady?"

Refraining from answering, Daniel didn't pick up the pistol but stood looking at it sitting on the glass counter.

"Only five guineas, sir. Very rare," the pawnbroker said.

"Where did you get this? Did a young lady bring it in?" Daniel looked directly at the man.

"I am unable to disclose my source, sir," he said, keeping Daniel's gaze.

Moving quickly, Daniel caught the man unawares as he grabbed him by the throat with his good arm, pulling him closer. "Now if you have purchased this legally, sir, you will have the name of that seller in your receipt book. I'd like to look at that book, understand!" Daniel growled.

Gasping, the pawnbroker straightened his hairpiece before attempting to speak. "I bought it in good faith. If it's stolen, I know nothing about it."

"I'm not interested in that. I just want to know the name of the person who brought it in. She may be in danger. Don't try my patience," Daniel stressed.

Grabbing the book, he looked at the few purchases on the current page. There it was, Hannah Church. She had received twenty-five shillings, less the cost on the day she had seen him in gaol. "Where did she go after this?" he said. "What direction did she take?"

"I don't know where she went, maybe she crossed the road. I closed the shop for the day after she left and I went into the office."

"If I find you have anything to do with her disappearance, I'll be back and you might regret that." Daniel walked toward the door. All he could confirm was that Hannah had sold the gun before returning to the gaol but he still didn't know what happened after that.

Stepping outside, he took a deep breath. His ribs ached after grabbing the man. He would have to be careful, he wasn't ready for a fight but fight he would if it brought Hannah home. Going into the Black Bull, he ordered a whisky which he downed in one. This helped ease the pain in his chest but not his confusion over Hannah's disappearance.

Ordering ale, he spoke generally to the landlord, explaining why he was in the area. He wondered if anyone had seen a young lady leaving the pawnbroker's on the previous Thursday afternoon. The landlord couldn't help but called his wife over. There had been a commotion on Thursday, she said. A woman had been arrested but she hadn't seen the affray though some of the customers had spoken about it. Mr Horsey, the pawnbroker might know as the constable escorted the young lady back inside the shop, she believed.

They stared as Daniel jumped off his stool, striding toward the door and almost knocking John over as the door slammed open.

"Watch out, what's the rush?" John yelled, jumping back and realising it was Daniel but he had to turn, running behind Daniel as they crossed the road between the cabs.

"That weasel of a man knows something," Daniel said, hammering on the locked door.

"Calm down, calm down. Let me speak to him," John said, trying to restrain Daniel as he continued to hammer loudly on the door. "Are you sure about this?"

"Yes," Daniel replied. "I saw Hannah's name in the receipt book and the landlady said there was an incident with the polis on Thursday."

"Move out of the way then, you're in no fit state to do this. May God forgive me!" John shoulder charged the door which sprang open.

The pawnbroker was snivelling in the office as the two men rushed in. Putting a hand in front of Daniel, John spoke quietly, pulling at his dog collar with his other hand. "I believe you have some information which may help find a friend of ours. Now this gentleman," he put his hand toward Daniel, "has confirmed with you that our friend did come here on Friday and we want to know what happened after you paid her for the pistol? You can give us that information of your own volition or this gentleman here," again he pointed to Daniel, "will have my permission to beat it out of you."

Daniel was still in shock by what John had done and didn't realise he was clenching his hands into fists.

The pawnbroker was shaking but replied, "I know nothing. I told him I don't know what happened after I closed up."

The man shrank back as Daniel moved toward him.

"People saw her come in here later with a policeman," Daniel said, "so what was all that about? I can go to the polis and find out but don't waste our time!"

"All right, all right," the pawnbroker said. "I don't know how much you know about this woman but she stole a ring from me and the polis were called. She was charged and I don't know what happened after that. That's the truth, now leave me alone."

"Hannah would never have stolen from you, I know that," Daniel snarled. "If I get no joy from the court, mark my words, we'll be back and woe betide you then."

Walking back toward the prison and court, Daniel let out a bellow of a laugh. "Well, John, not all goodness and light, are you? There's a darker side to you." He patted John on his back.

"Ouch," he replied. "I won't be doing that again in a hurry. I'll have a bruised shoulder, that's for sure."

Both were shocked to hear from the court that Hannah had been convicted of theft before being sent to Sheerness for a ship to Australia. For a short time, both were speechless, trying to absorb the information. Neither could believe what had happened. It was decided to spend the night at the Black Bull before getting the early train to London. They would somehow find transport to Sheerness from there. They booked rooms and sat in the bar, ordering food and drink. Both sat like old friends going over the day's events. They were both in agreement that Hannah wouldn't steal. Why would she? The pawnbroker had offered her money for the pistol so why would she consider stealing a gold ring? She already had a wedding ring which she didn't wear. They said the same thing in several different ways but couldn't come up with an answer.

"That man has something to do with it, I know. He's lucky we are off early in the morning or he would get another visit," Daniel said as he finished his ale.

"Yes, that's as maybe but let's remember why we are here. We need no more trouble as that won't help Hannah if we end up locked up," John replied.

"Going all holy on me, are you, pastor? Don't you forget I saw you break that door down."

Daniel laughed and John joined in with him.

Early the following morning, they were back at the railway station for a train south. Daniel admitted he had never been to London before, and John said he had only been twice. The two of them talked through various scenarios during the journey but none made any sense. Daniel said he would willingly change places with Hannah if this gave her freedom. John thought this was very Christian of him but wondered what was really between them. Daniel saw it as a way out. His life as he knew it was over. He didn't feel he could start again smuggling contraband in all weathers. Nor did he want to be cooped up in that house, even with Adele. Shaking himself out of his melancholy, he watched the scenery as it passed by the train window.

The journey was a long one which made it too late to consider continuing the journey the same day. Leaving the station, they saw in front of them a large red brick building, the Great Eastern Hotel. The reception had marble floors and pillars. Daniel had never seen anything like it, Italian tiles and marble with high ceilings and a stairway which seemed to rise to heaven. The whole hotel was very ornate and also very expensive which concerned him. Neither could dress for dinner so the two men walked along the streets until they found a small pie and mash shop. The number of people seemingly wandering aimlessly in all directions shocked both of them as did the hire cabs travelling on both sides of the road. The whole place was hustle and bustle and they were fortunate not to suffer injury as they attempted to cross the roads. Both were tired after the long journey and after arranging for a hackney cab to pick them up the following morning, they retired for the evening.

The journey, although uneventful, was a bumpy ride as all haste was required. It was early afternoon when they reached the port of Sheerness situated on the river Thames. John was adamant that he should do the talking because as a pastor, no offence, he would have more sway to gain information from the men in uniform.

Along the dockside, ships and boats of all shapes and sizes were anchored including wherrys which Daniel recognised. The shipping clerk confirmed that there had been a ship holding female convicts but it had sailed for Portsmouth that very day. He didn't have a list of names but would go and find someone who may be able to help. Impressed by John's quietly spoken words, Daniel shifted from one foot to the other, waiting impatiently. Finally after what seemed an age, a stout man in a naval uniform introduced himself as the shipping officer. John provided the man with Hannah's particulars and the man confirmed she was on board. He also confirmed that the ship would eventually sail to the colony of Australia.

Trying to explain to the officer, John said he was sure Hannah was innocent of the charge as the man shook his head. "I am sorry to hear that but there is nothing that can be done. The judge who would have sentenced her would have to provide a letter of pardon before the ship's captain would consider releasing her."

Both John and Daniel looked at each other. They hadn't considered that and felt their journey had been a waste of time. Eventually Daniel said, "We could go back to the court and ask for a pardon but we would need evidence that she was wrongly charged."

"I could vouch for her good character but I don't know what evidence they had to charge her," John admitted. "That pawnbroker must have had further involvement, of that I am now certain."

They said no more for a while as the cab rocked along the same road as they had travelled just a few hours before.

Breaking the silence. John said, "Perhaps you could enlighten me on why Hannah was at Stainsby Gaol in the first place?"

Pausing before replying, Daniel thought about his words carefully. "I was attacked by a gang and apparently Customs and Excise came upon me badly beaten with contraband. I was taken to the gaol but as they couldn't prove the goods were mine, I was charged as a debtor. I had no money to pay the debt but managed to get a message to Adele who went to Hannah for help." He knew he was being liberal with the truth but went on, "The rest you know as much as me."

"What I'd like to know is what you have to do with Hannah. Are you Daniel's father?" John was insistent.

"No, of course not. I would never have left her on her own if I had been. She was already pregnant when I came upon her travelling the road. I felt sorry for her and agreed to take her with me to Kingsmead, that's all." Daniel didn't want to continue with this conversation so closed his eyes, waking just before arriving again in London.

Rather than spending a further night in the capital, they took the mail coach which would get them back to Stainsby early on Friday morning. They agreed that they would try to speak to the judge about Hannah and they could make a decision after that.

Daniel and John stood outside the court waiting for the session to start. They wanted to try to gain an audience with the judge who had sentenced Hannah. The rain had been pouring down since they had arrived in the town, making them both look like bedraggled ragamuffins. The judge grudgingly gave two minutes of his time when he saw John's clerical collar but felt he was unable to help. He remembered the girl because of her eloquence on the stand. However, the evidence was stacked against her and he was not prepared to change the sentence even with John's character reference. Maybe a new life would be the making of her, he said as he walked away.

"We tried," John said sadly.

But Daniel blamed himself and it was clear to him that John blamed him too. The slight camaraderie of the last few days was lost as the practicalities of what to do next were discussed. John decided to return to Kingsmead immediately as there was nothing left for him to do now. He still had the rest of his parishioners to consider. He agreed to call on Adele to let her know what had happened and discuss the welfare of Hannah's young son.

Daniel wanted some space to deal with his angst so decided to visit James and Primmy for a few days after heading to the fens.

Shaking hands uncomfortably, they went their separate ways.

CHAPTER SEVENTEEN
JOURNEY TO THE ANTIPODES

Hannah was so distressed at the situation she found herself in that she took to her bunk for almost a week. She didn't eat or speak as depression overwhelmed her. Her new friends tried to rally her by bringing food and water but she pushed it away. They begged her to read to them but she closed her eyes as the tears slipped through her long eyelashes. It was the nights when she felt most alone when she cried silently for her baby who she was sure she would never see again. He had been the only light in her life and now that light had been extinguished. She couldn't bear it. Her heart was breaking. She had never felt such pain.

The women were shackled together each night by the wrists which gave the sailors the opportunity to rape them without much resistance. Some of the women accepted this was part and parcel of their life now. They attached themselves to one man who would then 'take care of them' for the journey. She couldn't do it, she just couldn't allow that to happen to her. She kicked and screamed as each one raped her until she had no voice. It made no difference to the sailors as they seemed to enjoy the fight, violating her in the most cruel of ways. Her wrists bled as she tried to free herself. She had a black eye when she was hit as her knee met one of the sailor's private parts.

The women told her to just lay back and think of something else then it would be over quicker but she couldn't allow it to happen without trying to defend herself. The smell of rum on the men's breath took her back to her dead husband and the cruelty in his hands. She had nightmares, crying out in the dark nights until the other women became annoyed with her. Death by hanging would have been better than this hell she was in now.

The gouge on her face and her bleeding wrists became raw and infected. She felt herself descending into a deep blackness but when she became delirious, the ship's doctor was called for. He was a young man on his first trip, keen to prove himself by ensuring no one died on his watch. He was sure the young lady was dehydrated so ordered copious amounts of warm sweet tea with a splash of lime juice just in case it was something more serious. Using some of the other women's pillows, he propped her up before spooning tea into her mouth. At first, she coughed and spluttered but he persevered until the liquid was swallowed. Her wrists were bandaged while he cleaned her face which was raw.

Mary, the young girl with the pock marked face, brought a warm cloth to wash Hannah's hands and face. The surgeon gave her the job of spoon feeding her the tea every half hour until the evening when he would be back to check on his patient.

The following day Hannah felt a little better but still didn't want to talk to anyone. It was Mary who eventually brought her from her malaise along with the surgeon. She told him that her body ached from the treatment by the sailors and she was worried she may become pregnant.

The doctor spoke to the captain about the probability of the women passing on sexually transmitted disease as the sailors took whoever they wanted on a nightly basis. The state of the convicts was of great concern to him, he said, and he was afraid many would die before reaching land. The captain wasn't a disagreeable man on the whole. He wanted an easy crossing though he did think the surgeon was a little wet behind the ears. It happens, he said, the men see a woman and it's primal instinct, the women were willing. The surgeon disagreed and after a heated argument when the surgeon banged his fist on the captain's desk, it was agreed that the sailors could only have sexual relations with the women if they were willing. There were enough of them who would entertain the sailors for food.

The young girl continued to bring drinks and small helpings of food to entice Hannah to eat. She bustled about, washing Hannah's face as well as cleaning her wrists by washing them in sea water before re-dressing them as the doctor had shown her. Each time, the young girl talked to Hannah about the new life they would have and how she wanted to be able to write her name. Mary begged Hannah to help with her letters so she could read, so she could have a chance that she had never had before. Hannah listened without speaking for a number of days until she realised that she did feel physically better. It would take longer for her spirit to heal. Patting Mary's arm, she said just said one word, "Tomorrow."

True to her word, the following morning with the aid of Mary, she rose from her bunk to wash and tidy herself. She almost collapsed at the exertion. Feeling weak, she managed to get to the kitchen where she sat with the others while they ate breakfast. The women she'd not seen before introduced themselves and it soon became clear that she would have quite a number wanting to learn their letters. Needing to keep her mind busy, she agreed to at least teach them to write their name.

Mary pushed her up the narrow ladder onto the deck to get some much needed fresh air. The sailors had left them alone and Hannah was relieved when her monthly bleeding came. It was late but at least she wasn't pregnant. The breeze was pleasant though cold as she stood holding onto the ship to balance. She felt her mind was somewhere else and without her thoughts of her son, she would have willingly thrown herself overboard.

On the ship were a number of Irish men who were keen to talk to Hannah when they were told she could read and write. They told her they were going to write a newsletter which the captain had agreed to and they had been given paper and pens. They introduced themselves as John Boyle, Thomas McCarthy, Mickey Phelan,

Dennis O'Reilly and William O'Connell. They asked her to write something for their pamphlet which she agreed to do, though she wasn't sure what she would write.

As the women were copying what she had written on her slate, she thought that it was less than two weeks since she had written the same on the board in Northend, her beautiful little boy covered in chalk dust. The thought saddened her but she shook herself. No more tears, she said to herself, just a steely determination to get back home to him.

Time seemed to pass more quickly when she was kept busy. It didn't give her time to think of the dire circumstances she found herself in. The women applied themselves to learning their letters in the morning after breakfast and the cleaning had been completed. Each day Hannah would go through the alphabet as the women recited it by rote. They would then look at the letters and try to write their names on the paper. They couldn't understand at times that their name wasn't spelt as it sounded but there was much laughter as Hannah wrote down their names to copy. She was a patient teacher, giving encouragement as the women became more confident and proud.

After a meal, usually bread with a little cheese or jam, they would go up on deck, sitting around Hannah as she read from the Bible. Her voice was clear as they talked about what she had read each day. One day as she took the steps down into the rooms, she heard someone imitating her words as she had taught the letters to the women. Walking quietly toward the room, she looked through the open door to see Mickey Phelan standing pointing to each man in turn as they laughed at his antics.

Stepping into the room, she said sternly, "Mr Phelan write out one hundred times 'I must not mock Miss Church'," before turning back down the corridor chuckling loudly. He wasn't bad with the mimicry. She would have to watch him. She might even write about it for the pamphlet.

That evening, she stood on the deck watching the sun drop into the ocean, arms folded against the cool breeze. It puzzled her where it went as it disappeared over the end of the world when the sea became a sombre black in complete contrast to the tentacles of red which spread out from the sun's rays. She felt rather than heard someone behind her but she continued to look at the fire of the sun on the water.

"I'm sorry for mocking you, Miss Church." Mickey tried not to laugh. Hearing the amusement in his voice, she turned intending to remain stern but when she saw the dunces cap on his head, her laughter was loud.

The others peering round the corner were also roaring with laughter. She realised that everyone else was making the best of the situation they found themselves in and she had to do the same before she went insane.

The frivolity continued as the sailors told them they were organising a party for the crossing of the equator, whatever that was, thought Hannah. The paying passengers were given seats on the higher deck away from the convicts who were crammed closely together at either side of the captain's upper room. It began in a similar vein to a play where the sailors dressed as women.

One took the role of Neptune who called forward those sailors who had never crossed the invisible line in the ocean. The novices including the doctor were initiated into the domains of Neptune. They were attached by a rope and beaten quite horrifically before the poor men were thrown overboard one at a time, dragged from fore to aft. They were hauled back on deck coughing and spluttering, half drowned. Everyone clapped and cheered as each one returned safely. Still attached by rope, the poor men were encouraged to walk the plank blindfolded as Neptune continued his play acting, prodding and poking the men. Others, including the doctor, were tipped into a large barrel of seawater where they were lathered on the face with pitch and paint before it was scraped off with a piece of roughened iron hoop.

The day culminated in a very wet slippery deck where they skidded and skated to great amusement. Mary grabbed Hannah's hands, pulling her toward the middle of the deck. Almost falling as her feet slipped under her, Hannah grabbed the nearest arm, the doctor's, who caught her around the waist. They both looked at each other somewhat embarrassed as she wriggled away.

The Irishmen made a wonderful newsletter full of jokes and caricatures of the sailors dressed as women. Hannah was impressed at the professionalism of it. She had written a piece about the difficulty of being a woman on board ship and her life before her conviction around the fishing village in Northend. She omitted to mention anything about her life as a married woman. The women were encouraged to talk about what they would like to put in the newsletter and she helped them to put it down in their own writing. They were all incredibly proud.

The journey continued in a routine for Hannah with teaching, reading and cleaning. Her busy days meant that she slept well each night but her prayers always included her son. She tried hard to remember what he looked like, wondering how much he would have grown since she last saw him. Even though it was only a few weeks ago to her it was a lifetime.

Christmas Day and New Year 's Day were really the only other days with a celebration which she wanted to remember to write to her son and tell him all about. An all denomination service on Christmas morning with hymn singing was uplifting even more than the usual Sunday service. After lunch they all sang carols and the Captain gave everyone a shot of rum.

Hannah declined, wrinkling her nose at the smell. At her prayers that night she hoped that little Daniel had been given a nice day and perhaps some contact with the other children. She didn't know who would be caring for him but hoped he was happy. She prayed wherever he was he was shown love and his pain in missing her would not be as great as hers.

The New Year of 1868 was also cause for great celebration and excitement that their journey was almost at an end. Mickey took the brave step of taking Hannah's hands in his. He had to tell her how he felt, tell her of his life before and his hope that the future would include her. After he had told his story, she told him hers. While they both knew there were no untruths exactly, they were both economical with the whole story. He asked if he had a chance with her, and said a maybe would suffice for now. Smiling, she told him she liked him well enough but wasn't sure what would happen once they arrived in the new land. Her main aim was to be reunited with her son. He had to understand that. Kissing her fingers, he promised to help her if she would let him though he knew he would never be able to return home.

There was great joy when land was spotted by the young boy in the crow's nest high above the sails.

CHAPTER EIGHTEEN
LIFE MOVES ON

True to his word, John called on Adele to tell her what had transpired. For her, it could not have been a better outcome. The woman had caused unrest between her and Daniel and now she was out of the way for good. Having the little boy with her meant she had some grip on Daniel who would surely be beholden to her now. As John took his leave, he asked Adele if she would consider bringing the boy to Sunday school so the parishioners could see him. He would also be very pleased to see her at church. She said that she would think about it.

Daniel took a train east before taking the carrier's cart through the small fen villages. The journey gave him plenty of time to think. He owed it to Hannah to be there for her son because it was his fault she had ended up at the gaol. Although he wasn't a religious man, he prayed she would be able to build a new life for herself as he would have to do. He wanted a drink, enough to blot out the whole sorry mess so he headed for the inn where he knew he would be welcome. His mood darkened when the landlord informed him that Laddie and Spot had died in the cart fire.

Although they had managed to escape when the flames took hold, it was the smoke which finished them off. Friends had buried them together near to Albarn Tamblyn's run down cottage. Pinto was being cared for so he needed to make a decision about what he was going to do with him. The innkeeper informed him that his uncle had died, never having really got over his injuries years ago and never returning to the wherry. Rumour was it was he who had given Daniel away and that came as no surprise to him. After much talking and drinking, Daniel struggled up the stairs to his room.

The following morning, he awoke with a headache. He went into the yard to swill his head under the cold tap. Sitting with the landlord eating a large breakfast, he discussed giving up his business as it would be difficult to start up again now he had responsibilities in Kingsmead. This surprised the landlord but he thought he might know someone who would buy the horse and goodwill from him.

Daniel found Pinto stabled a short walk from the inn with the blacksmith and promised to settle up for his keep within the next few days. Borrowing a saddle and reins, he rode with difficulty over to Albarn's old place. It was cold and damp with much of the remaining furniture damaged with water on the floor from a large hole in the roof. He had intended staying there for a few days but wasn't prepared for the tiredness in his bones nor his despair. He always thought he would be happy to spend his days here in his own company but now realised that he couldn't. After spending some time looking down on the small wooden cross at the dogs' grave, he got on with what he had come for.

At the side of the fireplace was a tin which held the last of Albarn's life. There was nothing of monetary value, a pocket knife and flint for starting a fire. Both he wanted to keep for sentimental reasons. Going to the well, his cold hands struggled to remove the wooden cover. He looked down into the dark void. Positioning himself over the gap, he felt around for the loose brick which he used both hands to remove. He could hear it scraping against the bricks on either side. Lifting it onto the top of the wall, he reached further into the gap to feel for the bag of coins. Sighing with relief, he pulled the bag, holding onto it tightly as it was heavy.

Taking it into the cottage, he tipped it onto the floor. Pebbles and stones spilled out, his money gone. Daniel put his head into his hands. He didn't know what to do. There must have been almost one hundred pounds of his life savings. Who had done this to him? Who knew? How on earth was he going to pay Adele the money back? He couldn't go back empty handed. He couldn't stand the shame. He sat until he began to shiver as Pinto stamped the frosty ground. He would have to sell the horse and business now, no doubt about it but he wouldn't get anywhere near what was in the bag. Rousing himself, he placed the tin in the money bag before pulling himself up onto the horse.

Later that evening, he drew up a contract with a keen young man who wanted to buy his business. He didn't have the full amount Daniel had asked for but the landlord vouched for him so it was agreed that he would leave money on a regular basis at the Green Man in Dealham until the debt was paid. He managed to pay in full for Pinto as well as a deposit and the two men shook hands.

At last, Daniel had some money in his pocket to pay for his vitals and bed at the inn which he paid for before going to the churchyard to visit Albarn Tamblyn's grave. Rubbing the top of the headstone, he said his final goodbye to the old man. It was with a heavy heart Daniel left the inn the following morning to make his way to Dealham as he wasn't ready to face Adele.

As usual, James and Primmy were pleased to see him. The inn was quiet and he was happy to get off his chest what had happened to Hannah and how it was his fault.

"Why didn't you get a message to me? I could have helped," James said as Daniel shrugged his shoulders.

Primmy was distraught when she heard that the little boy had been left behind. Poor little mite, poor Hannah, she wailed.

James patted him on the shoulder just as he had done with Hannah all those years ago. Daniel spent a week helping to tidy the cellar, move empty barrels and whatever they could find to keep him busy to cover his board and lodge. He spoke to contacts explaining his business sale and the young man who had taken over. James agreed to keep any monies for him until they saw him again.

Feeling refreshed, Daniel said his goodbyes before heading off to Kingsmead and Adele.

Both Adele and young Daniel were happy to see him but he felt lost. Being encased in this small house with no work made the days seem longer and longer. He had difficulty in sleeping, continually thinking of Hannah's wellbeing which left him moody. He realised he was better off in the company of men while he found it difficult making small talk with Adele. He certainly had nothing to say to Mrs Willows who thought she was the lady of the house even though she was contained in her room.

Taking pieces of wood, he sat by the fire like an old man, whittling, making a horse and cart for the boy as a Christmas gift. As the weather got colder, he realised his money and Mrs Willows' small pension would not provide enough food and coal for four people; there had barely been enough for two. As the man of the house, it was his role to provide and he had to do something about it.

He began getting up early before the rest of the house stirred to catch rabbits and wood pigeons to supplement the vegetables. He took sacks to collect wood for the fire which he dragged back to add to the coal, hoping to make it last longer. His hands were blue with cold, his hair soaking wet which dripped down his face and off the end of his nose.

No amount of begging or cajoling by Adele stopped him putting on his damp socks and coat each morning to get out of the way. Some of his afternoons were spent at the inn trying to make his ale last as long as possible. He wanted to drink himself into a stupor so he couldn't see the disapproval on Adele's face when he returned, arguing about spending money they couldn't afford. He tried to explain that this was the way he got the odd day's work with the drayman for a small amount of cash but she wouldn't listen.

Adele started going to St Nicholas Church each Sunday where John welcomed her warmly. Annie, Maggie and Nancy were delighted to see the young lad as he attended Sunday school with the other children. The few hours in other people's company became a welcome relief not only from her mother but also Daniel. They all struggled with the predicament at home, she knew how it looked. Her mother continually told her that it wasn't done to have a man in the house when she wasn't married and they were unchaperoned. Adele continually told her that it was Daniel's house so she couldn't ask him to leave and they had nowhere to go. Anyway, to all in the town Mrs Willows was a chaperone. It was her own fault she remained a prisoner in her room.

The mood was only lightened by the small boy's constant chatter and laughter. Adele found herself warming to him as her life seemed to focus around him rather than her mother. Christmas was a sober, sombre affair. New Year saw no celebration either, though they heard the church bells and boats on the river announcing the start of 1868.

About the same time Hannah arrived in Australia, Daniel's fortunes turned for the better. The whole household was woken early one morning by a banging on the front door. As he was still sleeping on the sofa in the small room downstairs, he pulled on his trousers before walking through the shop to the main door. A young boy hopped from one foot to the other with the cold as the door opened.

"Mister, mister, me dad sez can ye come, eh's 'ad an accident and needs yer 'elp."

Realising it was the coal merchant's boy, Daniel replied, "Go and tell your dad I'm on my way. I'll get dressed. Go on now."

Standing at the top of the stairs with the little boy in her arms, Adele asked what the commotion was and he told her. He dressed quickly, leaving by the back door and through the yard as he hurried to the coal merchant's.

The poor man had slipped on the cobbles the night before and when the doctor called, he was told his leg was broken. He would be off his feet for some time and needed help. He could see the predicament he was in but wouldn't be able to pay a wage as such but offered to provide Daniel with plenty of coal and logs. Daniel realised that the man was desperate to keep his business going but he was also aware that there were others who would be more than willing to help out.

Daniel agreed instantly and saw an opportunity which could help them both. Should Daniel find or increase business, he could keep the profit by buying the coal at cost price from the merchant. The coalman agreed to this as he felt that he already had most of the business in town so he wouldn't lose much if any money. He then gave Daniel a list of deliveries, what each customer required and the charge which he should extract before giving the coal. After giving Daniel his old coat and trousers as well as a hat with a large square of sacking attached to the back to cover his shoulders, the young son took him to the sacks and coal pile.

The coal merchant had only managed to fill a small number of sacks and place them on the cart before his accident so Daniel had to finish off the work before he could set off on the round. He found it really hard work shovelling coal into the sacks which he then had to hoist onto his shoulder to put them onto the cart. The dust made him cough, his throat dry. The man's wife brought him a mug of tea and a can to take with him and the young lad helped by filling sacks with wood.

Daniel enjoyed his day out in the fresh air even though there was a constant drizzle. He was good with the customers, managing to get a drink and at one place a piece of bread and ham. He was relieved as he had come out without any breakfast. This wasn't unusual but when he was last on his cart, he just sat while the horse did the work. Now he was jumping on and off the cart to deliver the coal and logs and as the day wore on, he became slower and slower.

It was a long day and he arrived back at the house exhausted. He had sluiced his face and hands under the yard tap at the coal merchant's before putting his own clothes back on but he was still filthy. Adele was aghast at the state of him, making him give his jacket a good shake before he came indoors. Even after he had scrubbed himself again with warm water and soap, the coal dust remained in the folds of his fingers and his nails but it didn't matter. He was happy after the few weeks trying to keep out of the way. Now he had an excuse and he was also going to make money. He was sure he would be able to.

Adele felt his new job was rather common. Why couldn't he find something better and cleaner to do? Maybe he could study like her papa to find an office post. Laughing out loud, he said he couldn't think of anything worse than being cooped up indoors and anyway he had never been a good scholar. His eyes had sparkled when he explained what had been agreed with the coal merchant. He was sure he would be able to set up his own business in the not too distant future. It would be a great opportunity for him, for them.

Working hard over the next few weeks, he took notes of the houses that he didn't serve as well as venturing further afield knocking on doors. He didn't want to step on anyone's toes but he was sure a deal could be made. He managed to increase the orders week by week. It meant really long days starting early to fill the sacks before doing the round. He spent the last light of the evening filling more sacks to try and get ahead of himself.

By the end of May, three things happened which changed Daniel's life in the strangest of ways.

The first was the sudden death of Mrs Willows. At first he was relieved that the old witch had gone but he didn't realise the effect it would have on Adele. He expected her to go into mourning black, which she did, but fell short of wearing a veil to hide her tearful eyes. What he didn't expect was for her to be so organised and matter of fact in arranging the funeral with John who it seemed had visited Mrs Willows on numerous occasions. The black bordered cards and notes with expressions of sympathy were sadly few as Mrs Willows had no friends or family to mourn her. There was a card from the ladies at the church and one from the pastor which offered sympathy but that was all.

The second was when two letters arrived on the same day. One was from Customs and Excise stating that Mrs Willows' pension would cease forthwith, leaving Adele penniless. She had expected it to happen but now she needed to plan her next action. The other letter was from Hannah explaining where she was and what had happened to her. The address was Cheapside Factory, Western Australia. Adele was tempted to burn it and say nothing but she had to be clever. Perhaps if Daniel realised how far away she was and that she would never come back, he would look more kindly on her. She would have to be wily to ensure they married otherwise she would be homeless and destitute.

The third thing to happen was when Daniel arrived home full of excitement so she didn't manage to tell him about the letters that day. Grabbing her hands in his, he told her what had transpired as he spoke to Mr Carter at the end of the day. The coal merchant had been impressed at his increase in work and asked if he would be interested in buying into the business so he could expand further. The downside was Daniel would have to purchase his own horse and cart. He thought he could sell the house they were currently living in which was most sought after, being close to the market square. There was a small cottage they could rent next to the coal merchant's. It would need work doing on it but it would be ideal, he said.

Adele sat with her hands still in his as she waited for him to finish. With an irritating calmness she said, "What do you intend to do with me, Daniel? Am I to be put out on the street with the boy?"

He assumed she would be happy to move with him and said so.

"It was one thing being under the same roof when mama was alive but my reputation would be lost if I now moved with you. I can't do it, Daniel, I really can't," she said somewhat dramatically.

Daniel tried to explain that he would need the money from the house to purchase a share in the business, it was the only way he could raise the money. The house would provide all he needed and more. He would be a partner in his own business and he would work hard to provide enough for them all.

Looking at him, Adele was waiting for him to say something about her but he didn't mention her predicament. In the end, she broke the silence. "There is one solution to this, though you may not want it."

He looked at her but still didn't speak.

"Do I have to spell it out for you? For goodness sake, Daniel, you could ask me to marry you. Is that so abhorrent to you?"

"But I need the money now, Adele. You are still in mourning and will be for some time," Daniel replied.

"That may be so but marriage would be more amicable than being thought of as a whore. Is marriage such a bad idea, Daniel?"

He couldn't speak as she rose. Taking the boy's hand, she walked into the scullery to get him a drink, her legs shaking. She had almost begged him to marry her, prostituted herself to him. It was obvious he didn't want to marry her. Daniel finally followed her into the small room and put his arms around her shoulders.

"I don't feel worthy of you. I wanted to prove myself to you before I asked you to be my wife. This doesn't seem right, Adele. Are you sure this is what you want?"

"Yes, I am sure," she said, deciding this wasn't the right time to mention the letters. They could wait. "I will speak to John tomorrow about putting up the banns. We could be married in a month. Would that be quick enough for you?"

"You are a wonderful woman, Adele. Have I ever told you that?" He hugged her but she remained quite stiff.

She knew she had got what she wanted but had Daniel? She had got her way but at what cost only time would tell.

John was surprised, no shocked, when Adele told him of her plans. While he was happy to officiate at her wedding, he wanted her to be sure that this was what she really wanted. Although she said it was, her eyes gave her away. John thought that the man seemed to have women falling over themselves to be with him but he couldn't see the attraction. He was rough around the edges and certainly no gentleman which would be more suitable for Adele's standing in the community. In deference to the recent death of her mother, they would not have a reception and only a small number of guests to the wedding itself. John explained that Daniel would have to come and see him later that day to complete the formalities.

As they were drinking tea, John mentioned that he had received a letter from Hannah who said she had arrived in Australia in January. She had written the same to Adele and Daniel about what had happened. Realising that John would probably mention the letters later in the day when he saw Daniel, Adele knew she would have to say something when she got home. She would have preferred to have waited until after they were married.

Passing the letter to Daniel when he got home from work, she watched as he read it several times, shaking his head. His reading wasn't the best but he got the gist of it.

"I can almost hear Hannah's voice," he said. "I knew that the pawnbroker was involved in her misfortune but what can I do now? We will have to write to her to let her know we tried to save her and that her son is fine."

Adele didn't respond but in her mind she was adamant she wouldn't be writing a letter to that madam.

Wanting a new dress and bonnet for her wedding day, Adele ventured into the front room of the house which was still a shop though she had not made anything for a long time. Looking through the few bales of material, her eyes were drawn to a pastel rose but decided on a foreboding grey, the colour of clouds before rain, which matched her mood. She found a couple of yards of lace and chose it for a high collar to hide her birthmark and decided she would place some around the cuffs. She always thought her marriage would be a happy affair with her mama and papa as she married a gentleman. Not gentry, no, she wasn't that stupid but it would be someone with prospects. Now she was getting married to a man whose hand had been forced, she knew that.

Her malevolence was to that woman, Hannah. She could barely mention her name. Daniel had never been the same since he had met her. Fingering the rose material between her fingers, she decided to use it to make a few flowers for the rim of her bonnet and ribbons. In mourning or not, people would talk but that didn't matter, she wanted some colour and joy on her wedding day.

The three weeks leading up to the wedding were extremely busy for Adele as she spent several days cleaning the cottage ready for them to move into. It had deep brick walls with wooden framed windows looking out onto a small overgrown garden which would be nice for the boy to play in. It had only one room on the ground floor which housed the fire range with a kitchen area to one side of the chimney breast. The opposite side had stairs to an upper floor with two rooms under the eaves. The small windows were at either side giving the bedrooms a homely feel, especially when Adele dressed them with warm coloured curtains. Once the furniture was in position, it would be their home.

The wedding itself was a quiet affair with Mr and Mrs Carter for Daniel, Maggie, Nancy and Annie for Adele. Daniel's sister wasn't able to make it but he seemed pleased about that. Some of the local children waited outside the church for the customary coin throwing. They had tied up the lynch gate until Daniel threw the pennies for them to release it. They all shouted and cheered as they raced around the floor to gather up the money. Maggie had offered to take young Daniel for the night but Adele was afraid he wouldn't be returned so politely refused.

Their first night as a married couple wasn't as either expected. For both, their lovemaking was perfunctory as she was very hesitant. He took her as was his right as a husband, she gave herself as was her duty as a wife.

CHAPTER NINETEEN
A NEW LIFE AT THE
BOTTOM OF THE WORLD

On the 9th January 1868, the ship docked in Western Australia and for most on board it was the beginning of a new life beyond imagination. The convicts remained shackled in the depths of the ship as the sailors bustled about lowering sails and pulling ropes until the ship eventually docked. They waited in the darkness until all the paying passengers and their belongings had disembarked onto the dockside.

It was only then that Hannah and the rest exchanged the metal bands around their wrists for coarse rope. She found she could rub the rope against her bound and bandaged wrists, and the physical pain was such that for a short while the pain in her mind abated. They were led, single file, down the gangplank where they were lined up on the dockside. Swaying with dizziness, her body couldn't seem to balance. It made her feel sick, just as it had when the boat first set sail. She was lurching like a drunkard trying to put one foot in front of the other. Everyone seemed to have the same problem after spending so much time trying to balance on a rolling ship. Hannah and Mary leant against each other while trying to focus on what was going on around them.

It was hotter than anything she had ever encountered as beads of sweat stood on her forehead before dripping down her face. It was rolling down her back and under her arms. She tried to wipe it but as quickly as she ran her sleeve across her face, it became wet again. Her scalp prickled where her hair was still sparse.

Hannah watched as men walked in all directions carrying goods which had just been unloaded, before sitting on the dockside waiting for the next job. Carriages were collecting people, carts loaded with boxes and baggage for those fortunate to have somewhere to go. The convicts were lined up with the men in several rows one side, the women on another as they were pushed and shoved quite harshly. Settlers and military alike prodded and poked the convicts with a view to take them to work on their lands or households. It frightened Hannah to see that many of them were taken away to Lord knows where and with strangers.

A large number of men including her Irish friends were rounded up by a man in a sweat-stained hat and heavy crop which he kept using around the convicts' shoulders to keep them moving. As they were led away, Mickey called to her, "I'll find you, Hannah. I promise."

She hadn't enjoyed the journey to this new land but preferred it to the fear of the unknown she was feeling now. Those who hadn't been bought for work were loaded onto carts. Hannah and Mary managed to sit together as they trundled out of the docks to the Cheapside female factory. Hannah tried to look around her to get her bearings and see where they were going. It was too late to try to escape now, she felt. After all, how would she manage to sneak onto a ship and return home without being caught and charged with trying to escape. It would be damning and certainly mean hanging.

Eventually arriving at the factory, the women were again lined up in single file while they were searched by a matron who removed any personal items. Fortunately Hannah had secreted her purse about her person and as she was on her monthly, the matron didn't look too closely about her. The rope straps were removed and she was pleased to receive a bundle of clean clothes as did the others. The clothes she was wearing were filthy and crawling with lice especially around the folds in her arms and behind her knees. Her body had blood spots where she had picked them from her skin. She realised why they had cut the women's hair so short before the start of the journey.

Hannah ensured Mary was beside her as they were led to wooden buildings which housed several sets of bunk beds. She whispered to Mary to get the top bunk next to her as they might be safer there. They lay the bundles of clothes on the bed, laughing at the two calico caps they had been given for everyday wear. She thought it would hide the patchy tufts of hair which had grown unevenly on the journey. The serge dress was similar to the one she had been given in Sheerness but the petticoat was a soft cotton material. The jacket was the same drab colour as the dress, the sleeves wide around the cuff. To finish the outfit off, they were given an apron which had a large pocket at the front. Hannah thought the Sunday clothing was marginally better with a white cap to go under a straw bonnet, grey stockings to wear with a pair of boots which would come as a welcome relief from the clogs she had been wearing for the last three months. She thought of her Sunday best from home, her need to feel self-important in front of Adele which seemed another life. The remainder of the clothes included a long serge dress with a muslin trim, a red calico jacket the same style as the weekday one, two petticoats and two shifts. To finish the new outfit was a long bag where she could place her clothes which would be placed by the side of the bed.

The one thing Hannah would have loved before replacing her clothes would have been a long hot bath where she could remove the remaining lice. How wonderful it would feel to wash her hair and body in warm soapy water instead of sea water which left a white covering of salt on the skin. The only washing facility she had seen was a stone trough in the yard but she had no towels or comb so her dream would have to remain that, just a dream.

She was shocked back to reality when a soldier grabbed her roughly by the shoulder which made her squeal in pain and shock.

"Get outside, you lazy scrubber," he said. "There's work to be done."

Pushing past him and grabbing Mary by the hand, she followed the other women back out of the wooden shed across the quadrant to another shed which was much larger.

Women were already sitting at benches, and the soldiers stood the new convicts alongside the women to learn the various jobs. Hannah was shown how to card wool ready for spinning. There were bales of wool in sacks all around the building which had to be carried to the benches by the women themselves. They didn't look too heavy but Hannah struggled to lift it to her shoulder and ended up dragging it across the floor.

She was quick to pick up the monotonous work which gave her time to think about her poor boy. Did he miss her? Was he crying? Did Adele care for him or was he living elsewhere? She knew that these questions would remain unanswered until she received a letter but she kept asking herself time and time again. The only way to keep her thoughts at bay during the day was to talk to the other women while continuing with her work, otherwise they were hit with a stick across the back of the neck by the soldiers if they were deemed slacking. Each day, she sat with a wooden paddle in each hand rubbing wool between them to straighten the fibres between the wire teeth. Her fingers were scratched and sore with the wire and her hands had become very dry. Eventually she realised the lanolin in the untreated wool helped if she rubbed it between her fingers before carding it.

The soldiers took an interest in the women for services rather than pay for a prostitute in the bars in town. Some of the women who had served their time or been left by a man had resorted to prostitution rather than destitution but Hannah was determined she would not go down that road. She made Mary promise they would go everywhere together as she didn't want either of them to be violated in this way. She knew she would not be able to take anymore. It had been bad enough on the ship and it seemed that she would never get away from men's pawing hands on her body. At night, she would pray to be kept safe as well as for the safety and love of her son. Hannah prayed asking God to be on her side and attended church every Sunday. This also gave blessed relief from the unwanted attention for a short while.

She had only been at the factory a few weeks when the warden ordered the women to line up in the yard as they had visitors. It was similar to a cattle market when men looked up and down the line occasionally stopping to look at a woman's hands or teeth. Hannah kept her head down, looking at her feet, not wanting to draw attention to herself. One of the men dropped a handkerchief in front of an eager young girl half his age who happily picked it up. She couldn't believe it when she was told they would be married almost immediately. The girl knew nothing of the man but it seemed marriage was the only way of escaping the brutal treatment in the hands of the soldiers. To Hannah, it seemed they could be exchanging one violent prison for another.

However she knew that it was only a matter of time before her or Mary were attacked or sent off with some undesirable. Hannah hadn't seen any of the men, especially Mickey, since they left the port and she had no idea where he had gone. She was beginning to think he would solve a number of problems and she liked him well enough. Did she like him well enough to marry him? Only time would tell, she thought.

Hannah was beginning to settle to her work during the day and continued helping the women with their letters in the evening. It had now become difficult to help with their reading because she only had the news sheets from the ship for them to look at. All of her students had worked hard and were now able to write out their name, of which they were all proud.

Early one morning before sitting in her position, she was called to the warder's office. Looking toward Mary, she was pushed in the back. Picking up the wool paddle, she placed it in her apron pocket. She crossed the yard between two huts and a soldier grabbed her, pushing her up against the wall. He propped his rifle against the wall and placed a hand over her mouth while pushing his body up against her. As he momentarily slackened his grip to unbutton his trousers, she grabbed the paddle from her pocket, hitting him hard at the side of his eye. Releasing her, he clutched at his head, blood trickling through his fingers. Hannah grabbed the rifle and screamed at him as he groaned before she ran toward the warder's office. Her legs were like jelly and she wanted to be sick. What on earth had she done?

The warder looked up as she rushed into his room, flinging the rifle onto his desk. They both jumped and fell to the floor as it went off, the lead pellet hitting the wall behind the warder's head. Almost fainting at the noise, Hannah took a deep breath before getting up, smoothing the front of her dress with her moist hands.

"Tell your men to leave the women alone," she screamed, thinking she would hang for this. "If anyone touches me again, I will not be responsible for my actions." Hannah held onto the desk as the injured soldier came into the room.

"Take your rifle and get out of here. I will deal with you later," the warder growled at the soldier. Waiting until they were alone, he laughed and said to Hannah, "You've got a temper on you, girl. I could charge you with stealing a rifle and attempting to kill me which could be a flogging at best or a hanging. What have you got to say to that?"

"Try it and I will speak to the governor. It was self-defence and your soldiers were in dereliction of their duty. I have nothing to lose, have I?"

Looking intently at her as if he was seeing the prisoners as human beings for the first time, he spoke again. "I believe you are teaching the women their letters. Is that correct?"

Hannah spoke clearly. "Yes, is that against the law as well?"

Ignoring the question, he continued, "There is a teaching post at the school which needs filling but the pay is low and not enough for a man to bring up his family. You can go into the community each day, returning to the factory in the evening. I have agreed this with the governor's office and your wages will be paid through me each Friday. Off you go and try not to get into trouble. This is a good opportunity for you."

Hannah knew he would take a cut from her wages which would go straight into his pocket. There would be no record of this, she was sure. As she took the dusty lane out of the factory toward the town, she had the urge to run but didn't know which direction she could go. She didn't want to be a fugitive forever and the scars on her wrists would always give her away as a convict who had arrived in this country in chains.

She was surprised to find that the town was only a mile or so from the factory so the docks could not be too far away. Smiling as she saw the small school, which reminded her of the one in Northend, she opened the wooden gate. It seemed the children had been left to their own devices for a number of days as the previous teacher had walked out, going into the interior to try to make his fortune. In order to engage the children, she lined them up tallest to smallest before asking their name and age which she wrote on the large blackboard. Several were from the same family. Picking on one of the boys who looked like trouble, she gave him the job of slate monitor. The smallest child became responsible for handing out the chalk.

It was a difficult first day as the previous teacher had not left any plans and she couldn't seem to find anything so she was glad when the day was over. She spoke to the only other teacher, Mrs Elizabeth Quinn, who was known as Lizzie and was a pleasant woman around the same age. They walked through the town together, chatting generally as they headed toward the small row of shops which she would have loved to have looked in but wasn't sure of the protocol. Yes, she was now a schoolteacher but she was wearing her prison garb so she would not be welcome. Saying goodbye to Lizzie, she continued back toward the factory.

Mary was on her mind as she walked back along the dusty lane. It had worried Hannah to leave Mary on her own as she had become fond of her. As the shops and houses disappeared, she heard a horse and cart behind her. Realising she was vulnerable, Hannah placed her hand into her pocket and felt the handle of the paddle which was a comfort. She picked up her pace in the hope that she would get to the factory turning before the cart caught up with her. Her heart was beating rapidly as the cart drew up alongside her. She was relieved when she heard an Irish accent, Dennis O'Reilly. Holding out his hand to help her onto the cart, they chatted as old friends trying to cram every word in before he dropped her off at the factory gates. He told her he was working on some land out of town with William and Thomas. Mickey was a loader at the docks and they saw each other often. Hannah asked if he would pass a message to him to let him know that she would be at the school each day during the week.

Waving until Dennis was out of sight, she realised how lucky she had been. Anyone could have come upon her. She felt more vulnerable here than she had on the first night on her own after she had killed her husband. It was strange she had not thought of that moment for a long time but this was the second time today. She had thought of that moment earlier in the day when the rifle had gone off. The smell of cordite and the fear of being raped brought back the consequences of what she had done all those years ago.

When she entered the bedroom, Mary and the other women rallied round her. They had heard the gunfire and when she hadn't returned believed that she had been shot dead. Mary had cried for most of the day at the thought of losing her best friend.

That night in her prayers, as usual she hoped her son was safe and happy. She also prayed that God would keep her from harm.

Her days were busy at the school but she was happy that she had made a new friend with Lizzie who told her that she lived in shared accommodation with her husband Adam who was a clerk at the court. They had also been sent to Australia as convicts several years ago but applied for a 'ticket of leave' and permission to marry which enabled them to work and live in the community. Hannah listened as her new friend explained the legalities as they walked from school each evening, realising that this could be a way out for her.

Hannah was beginning to despair of Mickey turning up when there he was cap in hand waiting by the classroom door as the children left for the day. His hair had a cowlick which wouldn't lie down no matter how many times he spit into his palm to moisten it, it was just there. It endeared him to her somehow and she smiled broadly. As they strolled along the road out of town, they talked generally before she boldly put her arm out to stop him.

"Are you still interested in marrying me?" she asked just as boldly.

Mickey pulled her close and whispered in her ear, "Of course I am. If you'll have me."

And so, the deal was done.

Hannah arranged to meet Lizzie's husband who would explain how to complete the forms to marry. The fact that they had travelled from England together would help as they could say they were a couple while on the ship. This would allow Hannah to continue to work as a teacher and live in a district of the colony agreed by the courts until her sentence expired or she was pardoned. Their 'ticket of leave', he told them, would require regular church attendance which she was happy with. What she wasn't happy with was that she would have to stand up in court in front of a magistrate. The one and only time this had happened was when she had been convicted and she didn't want anything to go wrong this time.

Around the same time Daniel and Adele were marrying in England, Hannah and Mickey were doing the same in Australia. The women found an old dress in the laundry so made a sort of waistcoat to go over Hannah's Sunday best dress and they embroidered the collar, cuffs and waistband with pretty cottons into flowers. One of the women gave her a sliver of perfumed soap to wash her hair and body making her feel better about herself. Her only regret at this time was leaving Mary behind but she promised the girl she would help as soon as she was able and they would see each other each Sunday at church.

Mickey turned and watched her as she entered the church, walking down the aisle alone. He thought her beauty was like a single flower in an arid desert. He loved her, he was sure of that but wasn't sure if she felt the same but he would do his utmost to make her happy. As she stood beside him, he could smell the heady scent of the magnolia blossom of the flowers. As she turned to him, she smiled weakly. Her thought was on the fact that she could be committing bigamy if her husband was alive but would anyone ever find out? She didn't want to hurt Mickey though she knew she was using him to keep herself safe but she had to survive at any cost to get home to her boy.

The couple moved into a single room of a house which was shared with a number of other families. A communal kitchen and outside toilet were on the ground floor. The only tap was in the yard so water had to be carried up several flights of stairs to the room. Both agreed that they wanted to save up to buy a place of their own so Hannah would work for as long as possible while living in one room at the top of the house near to the docks. The place insulted their senses with the stench of so many people living on top of each other as they spilled out of the rooms when the doors were open. Its smell hung in the corridors leading the nose up the stairs as though death was waiting.

The noise battered their ears as children screamed and women shouted at the same children while feet stamped on bare floorboards. Their tiny room was at the top of the house on the top floor under the eaves. In their room was one small window in the apex of the roof but it didn't open even if anyone could reach it.

Hannah was frightened when they were finally alone. She was frightened of being alone with a man and absolutely petrified of what he would do to her. She had explained to him about her husband's cruelty of her and he was aware of what had happened with the sailors on the ship. He hadn't realised that the same thing was happening at the factory with the soldiers over the last few months. Mickey promised he would never hurt her and never do anything she didn't want him to do. He ensured that their lovemaking was gentle, caring and kind. He never rushed her but waited until she was ready to give herself to him. It surprised her when she found herself looking forward to the intimacy of marriage. Mickey always held her tenderly after their lovemaking, his arms holding her closely, making her feel safe for the first time in years.

Hannah would have been extremely happy with her life with Mickey and her teaching but she ached for her son to be with her. She missed him every day, struggling to think how he was growing up. The children in her classroom changed each term and it was becoming more and more difficult to remember what he would look like. He would soon be starting school himself and not be the baby she imagined.

Three months after her marriage, Hannah found herself pregnant and they were both delighted with the news. She wrote to John and Daniel to tell them of her marriage and pregnancy. John had already responded to her previous letter which Mary had passed on to her and the latest one had probably crossed somewhere on that vast ocean. Now she was married and a teacher in the community, she could go into the post office without too many comments from the colonialist women.

As her pregnancy progressed, it spurred them on to find a place of their own. They had managed to save all her wages and she still had the money brought over from England. They hoped to find a better place before the baby was born. Adam and Lizzie who had become great friends often talked about trying to buy a place of their own but property within the town was hard to find and very expensive. Hannah broached the subject with Mickey one evening about how he would feel about sharing a property with their friends in order to get them out of the rental market. All agreed that it was a good idea so arranged to borrow a horse and cart to look further out of town for anything which may be suitable for the four of them to purchase.

The town of Cheapside had been built over the last fifty years around the dock area expanding into the outback as more people arrived. The main street with shops and houses continued along the road until the buildings at one end finished at the docks. Although rents were cheaper in this part of town, it was not an area for a couple to bring up a family. Sailors, soldiers and prostitutes alike lived and worked in the rooms above the inns as they could be rented by the hour or the day. The rooms above the shops were rented by numerous prostitutes and madams so were extremely busy in the evenings. Instead, the four of them took the cart in the opposite direction toward the factory prison but further into the area which hadn't yet been fully cleared.

It was like another world, the road being nothing more than a dirt track but every now and then posts marked out land that people had bought but not yet built on. They drove further out until it looked as though no one had ventured this far, no footprints, no pathways. They found a small property which looked derelict on a large plot of scrubland where trees and a stream formed a natural border. It wasn't so far out of town that they wouldn't be able to walk into work though Mickey would have the longest journey being at the opposite end of town.

The house wasn't so much derelict as unfinished. It seemed that someone had given up on it with the roof not completed, nor the veranda. Wood was piled next to the building ready cut in lengths ready to place on the roof trusses. Mickey looked at what was needed to make it watertight so they could live in it. The ground floor could be made into two sitting rooms with a shared kitchen in the middle. The staircase had not been completed but the men managed to climb through the gap into the first floor. It had no internal walls but they thought that they could make the roof space into three small bedrooms. Mickey believed that if they could get the place for a reasonable price, they could live downstairs for a few weeks so saving on rent while they completed the roof.

The windows would look out onto the unfinished veranda although they had no panes of glass just wooden shutters which they could close each evening to keep out the insects and bugs which were huge. They shouldn't really be called windows at all, just openings in the wooden frame of the house.

Mickey and Adam had so many ideas on what they could do to the place that the excitement rubbed off onto the two women. As long as Mickey was in charge of organising the physical side of things, Adam was happy to prepare the paperwork for the purchase of the property and land. They had to agree what they thought the house and land was worth but more important was how much they could afford to pay.

Adam struck a hard bargain with the governor's office when he provided the 'tickets of leave' to prove they were all eligible to own land and property. He completed the paperwork and within a few weeks they again borrowed a cart to take their meagre belongings to their new home. Apart from bedding and mattresses, they had just enough cooking utensils between them.

The first few weekends were hectic as the women collected wood for a fire to cook on and heat water from the stream to use for cooking and cleaning. The men climbed onto the roof, cussing and hammering wood to make it watertight. Each weekend and evening was really hard work but the four of them enjoyed each other's company and even more so because the work was for their own home. They finished each night when the stars came out and before they retired to bed, Mickey would stand with his arms around Hannah's waist looking at what they now owned.

She had never seen a landscape like it. Shades of brown ranging from light beige to mahogany as far as the eye could see. The soil had a red hue as the sun went down. Trees stood upright with no buds on twigs, no twigs on branches. Further away from the town was an impenetrable jungle where people disappeared, never to come back. The grass on their land was in huge swathes of long thin whispers, swaying gently in the breeze and reminding her of that dizzy feeling she felt when she stepped off the ship.

Mickey was always first off to work and last home. He would often carry pieces of wood or metal which he said would come in useful. He always seemed to know someone who knew someone who could help with a tool or idea. The blacksmith made spades as well as fashioning a hand plough to till the ground.

Adam didn't have the same physical attributes or technical brain as Mickey but was happy to be second in command doing whatever he was asked to do. Mickey would often have to explain several times before Adam got the gist but they laughed together. Adam would try and make up for his weakness by starting work the minute he got home in order to try and keep up. Hannah and Lizzie pulled up weeds, carried stones, and found brushwood for the outdoor fire as this was the only source of cooking and heating water. They would carry pails of water to fill the barrel which they had acquired from the docks and placed beside the house.

Mickey would also bring home fruit and vegetables when a crate was broken open, helping their scant diet. Much to the delight of the women, he arrived home one evening with a box on his shoulder holding a dozen chicks. A hastily-built hen house was made from a crate to keep them safe. They were thrilled that, in a few weeks, they would have their first eggs.

Clearing the scrub was backbreaking work especially on Hannah who was now heavily pregnant. Roots seemed to go to the centre of the earth as they hoiked weeds and grasses. Once they had cleared a big enough plot, they began to sow wheat and vegetables, the seeds also coming from the docks in Mickey's pockets. It was difficult to know what some of them were, so they were delighted when small shoots began to appear.

Spring and summer saw the bare dry land changing into a vibrancy of colour which was beyond comprehension. The trees became a canopy of leaves in all shades of green with blossom in pink and white. Hannah could not believe the rainbow colours of the birds which she learnt were parakeets in blues, yellows and greens in flocks of hundreds roosting in the trees. They were small, a little larger than a sparrow but made a cacophony of noise night and morning.

The shoots of green in the vegetable plot seemed to grow bigger every day in the warmth of the sun but they required copious amounts of water. There was a quiet excitement at the thought of picking a mixture of vegetables to eat. The ears of corn were turning from green to cream to yellow as the grain was almost ready for picking.

One afternoon, Hannah thought she could see snow in the distance, calling to the others to come and look. She hoped it would cool the oppressive heat which she had struggled with during the latter stages of her pregnancy. How wrong she was as they all stood watching the white haze travelling toward them. It was a plague of insects where no amount of swatting or wafting slowed them in their savagery as they decimated their crops. Hundreds of the insects fell out of the sky, too full to fly off and destroy other vegetation. They were swept into piles as they died on the ground. It was the numbers and speed which was the most frightening. They got into hair and clothes as they all tried to wave them away from the wheat. Hannah looked at them by her feet. Nature was strange. These creatures were in some ways beautiful with lattice wings as fine as lace. They were a most wonderful shade of green with black and red markings.

Hannah and Mickey sat on the veranda steps, arms around each other watching the sun go down. They couldn't speak as they looked at the devastation. After all the hard work, they had lost everything in just a few hours. The birds were chirping loudly the following morning as they ate the remaining seeds. It was a disaster for the four of them. They needed to produce their own food to survive for the rest of the year.

Hannah knew they would struggle financially as she was almost on her time and her wage would soon cease. Even though it was a miserly amount for the work she was doing, it had helped them to get on their feet. She had an idea although now wasn't the best time to discuss it.

The early hours of 18th August 1869 saw the birth of her second child which was much less traumatic than little Daniel's. Yes, she said it was very painful and she screamed loudly with each contraction and push. Lizzie encouraged her, holding her hand just as Annie had done the first time. This time she knew Mickey was pacing up and down outside the bedroom which gave her some comfort. They both cried when she produced a daughter which she named Amy after her mother and Rose because of her tiny rosebud mouth. She had a mop of dark hair just like her father's and eyes the deepest shade of blue. As she held Amy Rose to her breast, Hannah vowed she would never leave this child. How she wished her first born was here to see his baby sister.

When Amy Rose was just three weeks old, Hannah spoke to Mickey about Mary who he remembered from the days on the ship. Mickey knew what had happened to Hannah and how she cried when she thought that Mary might be suffering the same fate. He relented when she told him about her promise to help the girl and her plan which would enable her to return to work so they would have some money to plant more crops and put money to one side to send for her son.

Hannah had to wait until Saturday to take the long walk to the prison carrying Amy Rose in her arms. Lizzie had offered to care for her but she hoped the child would help in the release of Mary.

Demanding to see the warder, she explained to him that she needed a nursemaid, requesting young Mary. Placing five shilling on the desk in front of her, she stated this was a fair price for the girl's release as she would need training. The warder blustered, scraping back his chair and Hannah saw the hole in the wall where the lead pellet had landed all those months ago. He knew she was a formidable woman but said he would require double that amount to even consider releasing one of his convicts. Standing her ground, Hannah spoke quietly, stating that she had no compunction in talking to the justice about his monetary dealings which she was sure were not legal as was taking a portion of her wages prior to her marriage. The five shillings would end up in his pocket because she had taken legal advice and knew there was no charge for a genuine post and this was what she was offering. Hannah was thankful that Adam had been able to give her limited information on the subject, the rest she would brazen out.

When Amy Rose started crying, Hannah didn't try to comfort her but let her cry. It unsettled the warder as he shouted for one of the guards to go and find Mary and bring her back to the office. His shouting caused Amy Rose to cry even louder which upset Hannah but she didn't look at the child. Mary heard the cries and knew it would be Hannah. Rushing up to her, she flung her arms around Hannah and the baby.

Hannah smiled. "I'm taking you with me to live with my family as a paid nursemaid. Is that alright with you, Mary?"

The girl clapped her hands with joy, signing her name proudly in the register before being handed a piece of paper, her freedom.

Mary rushed off to get her Sunday best clothes and boots before joining Hannah at the front of the factory. Hannah smiled as they walked out of the gates together and even Amy Rose stopped crying. They walked back to her home while Hannah explained what she would like Mary to do. The idea was that Hannah would return to work at the school each morning while Mary remained at home with Amy Rose. At midday, she would carry Amy Rose to the school so Hannah could feed her and Mary could remain in the class in the afternoon to continue with her learning before returning home together. Mary could not believe her luck and said so many times before they reached the house. Mickey had hugged her when he arrived home from work while Adam and Lizzie made her feel welcome. It was like the family she had never had, Mary told them around the evening meal.

Life was almost perfect for Hannah and if her son had been with her, it would have been. She realised that there were so many more opportunities in this new country if you were prepared to work hard. After all, in England she would never have been able to purchase a house. It was so cheap compared to properties at home.

Home? She would never go home now. This was where she belonged with her husband and daughter and, one day, her son.

She wrote again to John and Daniel though it was only John who ever responded but he did keep her up to date with what was happening to her son. She was pleased that little Daniel was going to church and meeting up with his extended family. John told her that the lad was happy and growing fast. Adele was looking after him well, which made Hannah happy.

Amy Rose was almost a year old when Lizzie said she was expecting, much to the delight of Mary who found she was a natural with babies and hoped she would be a nursemaid to the new child.

The men were in a great rush to plant more wheat and vegetables as the number in both families increased. Hannah talked about the fishing nets she had repaired in Northend. She thought something similar could be used to protect their crops. She had never been very good at repairing them but she was sure she could do something. The men made up a wooden frame over the seeds as the women watched Hannah make the holes in the netting smaller with a handmade wooden needle. The net of course had come from the docks, thanks to Mickey.

Amy Rose was not yet three when Hannah gave birth to another daughter who they named Kathleen Jane to be known as Kitty. The new daughter was named Kathleen after Mickey's mother and Jane because they both liked it.

She wrote to John and Daniel to tell them the good news but

again it was only John who replied. Hannah realised Daniel might not be able to write and perhaps Adele wouldn't. After all, they had never been friends. In fact, they really hadn't liked each other at all. However Hannah hoped that she would eventually receive a letter from her son which she would treasure. It was enough to know Adele was caring for her boy who would now be at school. One day, Hannah kept telling herself, he would be here and her family would be complete.

Life continued with Mickey working at the docks and Adam in the court. Lizzie had returned to work after the birth of her son, Joshua. Hannah talked to Mary about looking after three children, as she felt it could be too much for her. Amy Rose was now three and becoming a proper little madam. She bullied Joshua who was almost two, as well as making a nuisance of herself when Kitty needed attention. Mickey didn't want Hannah to return to work, saying that his daughters needed their mother at home. Hannah wanted to spend more time with her children especially as she was breastfeeding Kitty. Mary wouldn't be able to bring all three to the school as she had with Amy Rose.

Hannah reluctantly agreed to stay and help with the children but she worried about the money situation. Life would be a struggle, even more than before so she tried to work on the land some of the day while making the evening meal for when they all got home. Mary was still given a small wage which she saved for the days when she went into town where she spent it on ribbons or fruit for the children. The men still worked hard to produce food, planting and drilling at weekends while the women still attended church each Sunday. There were times when Hannah had to dip into her meagre savings to top up their income and she was disappointed when she could see that little Daniel would never be with her. Her life would have been perfect if he had been with her.

But Hannah's life was to fall apart when Kitty was eight months old and Amy Rose was four. Mickey and Adam had spent their free time clearing more land ready for planting winter crops. Mickey came in one night complaining of a pain in his leg after being bitten by something. He had a red mark on his calf which seemed to be getting bigger. He thought it might have been a spider bite. Over the next few days, his leg became red and swollen until he could hardly walk. He struggled to get to work. In the end, Hannah made him stay in bed, giving him plenty of water though he was constantly being sick. Mickey also complained of a headache. Hannah sat up with him, trying to cool him down but by morning he was delirious. She had nagged him to go to the doctor but it was obvious that the doctor would have to be called to the house. Mary ran to the town to ask him to call as soon as he was able.

Sadly by the time he got to Mickey, he said there was nothing he could do for him except try to make him comfortable. The poison had got to his nervous system, he said, and even if he had seen him immediately, he couldn't help.

Hannah paid the doctor then returned to sit with Mickey as his life slipped away. She told him she loved him and that he had made her very happy but in the early hours of the morning, he slipped away. She was bereft. Her life meant nothing without him. He had been her rock in this new land. Her children had lost their father. Kitty hadn't even really got to know him.

The small amount of money she had left, she used for his funeral. His Irish friends dug his grave in the corner of their land where Hannah wanted him to lay. He was close to the trees where he had spent a lot of time. Hannah placed a wooden cross at the top where she placed flowers, or weeds which had pretty colours. It was a place where she would sit and talk to him with the children or on her own. She descended back to the place she had been when she had been sentenced all those years ago. When she had lost her son. It was her fault and she knew it. God didn't think she deserved to be happy.

It was three months before she could put pen to paper to write to John and Daniel to tell them what had happened to Mickey. What she didn't write was that she was sure God had yet again punished her for being happy as a consequence of her murdering her first husband. Now her children had no father. He would never see them grow into young ladies, never see them marry and that was all her fault. Her grief was palpable but again it was Mary who helped her through, quietly caring for her and the children, holding her when she cried and leaving her when she walked to Mickey's grave.

Hannah felt her life was over. Even the children didn't release her from this malaise. She had learned to love Mickey who was a good husband and a good man. Now he was gone. This time God was punishing all her children for her actions and she didn't know how to cope with it.

CHAPTER TWENTY
MAKING A DECISION

Daniel read the letter over and over again. He couldn't believe it. Poor, poor Hannah. What was she going to do? A widow with two small children? Two babies? How on earth would she manage with no breadwinner? Hopefully, the friends she had in Australia would rally round and help her in her despair. The letter was still in his hands when he was brought back to the present by Adele's harsh voice.

"She's not having him, I tell you. She abandoned him when she left him with me. I'm his mother."

"Adele, stop it!" he said. "You're not his mother, he has a mother. Anyway, it will be years before she can afford to send for him. By that time, he will be able to make up his own mind."

On and on it went and Daniel just couldn't stand it. He was a coward, he knew that. Picking up his jacket he called to the boy to come and help him with the horse. The lad was now over seven years old and at school. He was clever but Adele had him like a pretty boy with his clothes and long curly hair. She didn't like him to get dirty. She kept him like a girl but Daniel had stopped telling her she was making the boy soft, a cissy. He would grow into a milksop who wouldn't be able to do physical work. She blamed him for not having children of their own. Each month for the first year of their marriage, she had tears and tantrums when she found she wasn't pregnant. It didn't matter what he said or did, her comments were acerbic so he almost gave up talking to her. He must have been out of his mind marrying her but what could he have done? Had he ever really loved her? He thought not. He wanted her because he thought he would never have someone like her. He wanted some standing in the community which he thought she would give him. Too late he realised that wasn't the case.

Her mother thought she was someone and had brought Adele up to think she was better than everyone else but she wasn't. She had a mouth like a fishwife when she argued.

Daniel thought he had worked hard to provide for her and the boy but she seemed to resent everything he did. Nothing was ever good enough for her. The house was too small, she was too far out of town and she had no friends. Maybe she should look at herself over the last one. She wasn't easy to befriend. She was too much like her mother. She always stiffened when he tried to hold her and Daniel had given up trying.

Adele was preparing the evening meal, thinking along the same lines. Where had it all gone wrong? She blamed that strumpet. His head had been turned by her. Now she was writing saying her husband was dead. Well, didn't she say the same thing about the boy's father? She was probably never married to either of them. If she thought for one minute she was getting her son back, she would have a fight on her hands. She would talk to John about it, she decided, when she saw him the following day as she was sure he would also have received a letter.

Since the boy had started school, she had helped by visiting the sick at the workhouse hospital. She would help those who needed feeding as well as reading the Bible to others. It made her feel virtuous while being coy with John. He would have made a better catch. Her mama would have approved of him, that's for sure.

After they had eaten and the boy was in bed, Daniel sat by the fire with his pipe, eyes closed, waiting. Sitting opposite, Adele took up some sewing. "What does she want us to do? Send her money to come home? Why can't she just leave us alone?"

Without opening his eyes, Daniel said, "Hannah, her name's

Hannah, and I'm sure she doesn't expect us to do anything of the sort. She just wants to know how her son is and to tell us her dreadful news."

"Oh well, you would take her side, wouldn't you," Adele retorted. "I can't say anything about her at all, can I?"

"Adele, just shut up. You know Hannah is in Australia because of me."

Before she could say anything more, Daniel snapped, "I've had enough. I'm going for a drink."

Walking through the streets, it was early evening and still light. He couldn't stand it. His home life was miserable. He had been happier on the road. His business was going well and he had plenty of work. He worked hard to provide for them and he never left Adele short of money. Was he a weak man to just put up with it? He knew of men who beat their wives, just took them when they wanted but he couldn't do that.

By the time he had downed a few ales and chatted to the men in the bar, he made a decision. For the first time in years, he was going to be a man and make his own resolution to the predicament he found himself in. Now all he had to do was put it into action.

Before he returned to the cottage, he went into the stable and put one or two things together ready for the morning. He returned to the cottage and sat in the chair as he waited for Adele to retire to bed. He sat with the candles flickering in the draught. He wasn't very good at writing and he wanted to think of the right words before he put pen to paper. Dipping the pen into the inkpot, he wrote his first letter to Mr Carter. He explained he was going away and would be handing his share of the business to Adele and she could sell it or pay someone to run it for her. The rent on the cottage could continue to be taken from the profits until she wanted to move out. He apologised for the short notice and finished by thanking him for his faith and kindness toward him.

The letter to Adele was much harder to write but Daniel had to give an account of himself. He started by saying he was sorry that he hadn't been able to make her happy and that he had known all along that he wasn't good enough for her. It was cowardly of him not to talk to her face to face on his decision to leave but he was taking the boy to his mother where he belonged. He also explained what was in the letter to Mr Carter.

Wishing her happiness and hoping she wouldn't think too badly of him, he told her this was something he felt compelled to do. He signed it Daniel before taking off his wedding ring and placing it on top of the letter.

He sat long into the night, watching as the flickering fire died into embers and the candles went out before he stirred himself. He packed clothes into a bundle for the two of them before counting money from the tin on the mantelpiece, leaving enough to keep Adele over the next few weeks. He placed the rest in his jacket pocket. He wasn't sure if there was enough to get them both a berth on a ship but he would try to work his passage if he could. That way, he would have something to give Hannah.

Creeping up the ladder to the bedroom where Adele was still sleeping, he continued to where the boy lay. Daniel woke him gently, putting a finger to his lips as he wrapped the boy in a blanket and placed him over a shoulder, retracing his steps quietly. The poor boy was still half asleep but fortunately made no sound.

Picking up the bundle of clothing, Daniel closed the door as silently as possible and headed to the stable. He dressed the boy quickly and placed the bed clothes into the middle of the blanket. He then placed the bag of coins he had hidden in the stable on top before knotting the ends of the blanket together. Indicating to the lad to remain quiet, and carrying the bundle in his hands, they walked quickly toward the station for the early train to London and beyond.